DEADLY DUPLICITY

by

Struan Robertson & Anne Harling

CHAPTER ONE

It was busy the first time Caroline walked into the bar, but Roy picked her out right away. She'd hoped not to be noticed so quickly, wanting time to look round, to take the measure of the place, but when she turned to glance at him, he was already nodding at her over the press of people along the bar. A welcoming smile that asked her what she wanted to drink.

It wasn't her good looks that had brought her zooming into focus through the frenzy of a late night tourist bar in the grip of the Spanish holiday season, but rather her very stillness that made her stand out from the crowd. Roy instantly put her down as someone of note – someone special. He kept turning back to her in the brief snatches between clamouring customers.

Caroline waited, making Roy look directly at her before she moved in to the counter, declaring herself a customer. She'd taken great care with her initial approach, not wanting to come over as too forward. In the few seconds since entering the Winking Frog, she'd marked Roy down as a traditionalist – which for her, was another word for chauvinist.

Taking a seat at the bar, she glanced away for a second before bringing her eyes back slowly to meet his. Her gaze was steady and she kept it full

1

on him. It was a good performance, maybe too good because Roy now knew she was after something – and it wasn't the beer she'd ordered.

As he turned away to rake amongst the bottles deep in the dark beer cooler, she gave the bar itself a fleeting scrutiny and by the time he emerged with her drink, she'd seen all there was to see.

Not much, she concluded. A shabby little place, drearily typical of a hundred other expatriate tourist bars, tricked out with the memorabilia that was such a staple of these places, it could have been any of a dozen other joints along the strip.

As he turned back from the cooler, she had to resist laughing in his face, the smirking author of this dog's breakfast of a bar. He was almost too perfect for the part, she thought. Emma had obviously retained her sense of humour when selecting him.

Former wide boy, sometime smudger snapping Japanese tourists at the London Cenotaph without turning the film on until the digital camera put him out of business, Roy saw himself as rather special. It was an opinion not widely shared, so Roy had learned to keep his past to himself. Rita, his wife, knew exactly who he was, of course, but then she knew everything – or thought she did. Roy was glad she'd gone.

'Here on holiday?' Roy tried the standard opening. Caroline nodded as she took a swig straight from the bottle, preferring to take her chances with the bacteria from the bottling plant.

'Yes, a couple of weeks. My cousin and I thought we'd give Spain a go this year.' Her tones were neutral, middle-class and middle England.

Roy nodded as he swept her unused glass back below the counter. 'Good choice. Better than down

2

the coast. It's less crowded here. Less Club Sangria and Shag, if you know what I mean.'

'And you run the bar yourself. It's yours?' Caroline smiled to soften the apparent brusqueness of the question.

'Yes, me and the wife. Started it up a couple of years ago. Bought it as a shell. Fitted it out ourselves.'

'So, it's all your own work?' Caroline swung round to acknowledge once more the worn Formica, the gaudy strip lighting. 'Quite unique, really. You must have a good eye…'

Stopping herself before she went too far, she turned back with a wide, disarming smile. 'I could never have done it - and that's the truth.' The literal truth, as it happened.

Roy looked around obediently, noting his good taste once more. For a start, nobody else had a genuine donkey collar, not in the whole strip.

As neither seemed sure what to say next, Caroline picked her bottle up and sauntered around the perimeter of the bar, giving her undivided attention for a moment to a drooping notice board tiled with snaps of the regulars, clinging to each other in drunken comradeship. It was really no worse than she'd feared, but now it suddenly became more daunting. She waited a few moments longer, as she dealt with these conflicting emotions, before turning and strolling back to the counter.

Hitching herself on to a stool, she asked, 'And where is the lady wife?' Caroline always believed in getting into the part.

'She's away at the moment. Gone back home. Her mother's not well.'

Caroline nodded. 'So, you're here on your own.' It came across as a question. '…and you can

3

cope okay? I suppose you have some little senorita who comes in when it's busy to help out?'

'No. I do it all myself. That's the beauty of this bar. It's very compact and handy. I designed it like that so no matter how busy we get; one person can manage it. Mind you, you have to go at a fair lick at times, just to get round everyone. But in any case, I'm pretty fit.'

Caroline studied him. He did not look particularly fit. Not young or fit. If he was still in shape, she couldn't see where as he seemed to be disappearing into unfocused middle age.

'Okay,' she began suddenly, as if concluding something. 'Got to unpack the bikini and the toothbrush. See you later.'

She slid off the stool. 'You will be open later?' she asked, turning back to look at him.

'Yes, right through until four. It's coming up to the high season now, so we have to hit it while it's hot.'

Roy watched her go, his mouth slightly ajar. 'Now, that's a bit of class,' he thought as he turned back reluctantly to business and to the bottle cooler, fishing about in its innards looking for bottles of beer.

The cooler was a dangerous grotto. He should have emptied and cleaned it in the off-season but hadn't got round to it. Then, a couple of weeks ago, he'd cut his hand quite badly on the jagged stump of a broken bottle. It had needed stitches. Now, the more fastidious of his customers were remarking on his increasingly grimy and heavily bandaged serving hand.

The trouble with this bottle cooler, Roy thought, was that it was too dark inside to see what was going on. The bar itself was dark, but then it

4

had to be, not only for ambience, but to hide the slowly accumulating grim the years brought – and anyway, cleaning out the cooler was something Rita should have seen too; but then there were a lot of things she might have done. Now she had gone.

Straightening up while automatically clipping the top off a beer bottle, his mind was still on his wife. She'd disappeared four days ago. Nothing suspicious, because all of her gear had gone too, plus her passport and Spanish residence permit. Taking those said she intended to be gone for a while, if not for good. But then again, she had not left a note, although admittedly, she wasn't a note person.

They hadn't been getting on recently – but not bad enough, he thought, to justify her going off without a word. Half the business was legally hers and she took an active part in its running. That was what was so strange about it. It was definitely not like her. If he didn't hear from her soon, he'd have to make a few phone calls, see if he could track her down. She'd most likely gone back to London, her hometown – and his.

CHAPTER TWO

That evening the Winking Frog became busier as more people came in, some wanting food – which Roy had to turn out single handed. The business didn't run to hiring help, except on weekends at the height of the season. So, he did simple stuff, fat puffy pizzas in a special electric oven and toasties on the plancha. It was good for business, kept his customers in the bar, stopped them going off elsewhere to look for food half way through a boozy evening.

The dark lady came back later; it was well after one by then. This time she walked straight up to the bar and stood directly in front of him as if to say, 'Here I am!' while making an elaborate point of examining the food – slabs of corpse white bimbo bread and factory ready pizza that sizzled and spluttered in the darkly baroque interior of the electric oven. Then she turned back to say she was sorry, but she hadn't realised he did food or she wouldn't have eaten earlier.

Roy, recalling her apprehensive first glimpse of the little kitchen through a gap in the stained curtains, saw she was being polite. He'd heard it all before. He was already thinking of her as 'his' customer, something all bar owners on the costa did; if anyone came in twice, they were considered franchised.

Often after closing, Roy would go around the late bars, the ones that stayed open until the sun rose, on the pretext that he needed air. But really it was to see who was being unfaithful to him and sometimes, if business was really bad, he'd not wait until they'd closed, but leaving his wife behind the bar, would go off to look for them, his missing customers.

Then coming on them, he'd very ostensibly buy them all drinks, making a lot of fuss while enticing them back to the Winking Frog. He called it 'punter hunting,' and considered he did it rather well, rather subtly - but not many were taken in and it certainly didn't make him popular with the other bar owners.

But it was necessary, especially when business was bad, which seemed to be most of the time nowadays. Roy rationalised it simply as keeping track of his missing customers – and in crude economic terms it had to be done if they were to make it to the next season, through the long, empty winter months.

Now this good looking female was standing in front of him apologising for not having dined on one of his special pizzas – there was definitely something going on here. Having picked up on her the moment she'd walked into his joint, the signals were now coming through even stronger.

But he had no time to take it further now. There were twenty other customers ranged along the bar, every one British and all of them vying for his attention, to order drinks, to ask him things, to tell him jokes. They took as proprietorial an interest in him as he did in them, which meant he couldn't go off line for one moment. It was all part of the weary and wearing symbiosis between a costa bar owner and his customers and it was turning Roy into an old man before very his eyes.

His customers all had to feel they belonged, to be remembered beyond the brief weeks of their annual holiday. They would send Christmas cards; some even knew their birthdays and joke cards would arrive. And then when summer came round again, more postcards to announce their imminent return for another sun-soaked two weeks, saying exactly when they'd arrive and asking if Roy and Rita wanted anything brought out from England.

They would always say yes – for tea bags or pork pies, something small, something British and something they almost invariably did not need. It was all available in the local British supermarkets, but was simply a way of ensuring the punters came into the Winking Frog on their very first evening back in town, to catch them first and make them regulars again for the next week or so.

Coming out of his reverie, Roy gave Caroline a guarded smile and gestured down the bar.

'I have to go and serve them. What did you want?

'A large glass of white wine. A spritzer will do. Must take it easy, I want to hang on to what little sense I have.'

'Oh I'm quite sure you have plenty,' he retorted, a hint of sarcasm. 'I think you're being too modest.' And he made her the drink and still smiling, hurried off down the bar to join a group who wanted him to guess how many Irishmen, or Italians, it took to change a light bulb.

On his return, Caroline was idly leafing through a magazine as brown and curled as the cheese toasties sputtering quietly on the old black plancha next to her.

'So, you're here for a couple of weeks, you and your cousin?' said Roy, taking up the conversation again.' Is she coming along later or has she gone to bed already?'

'HE, actually! He's a he and he'll be along later, unless he gets waylaid somewhere else.'

She stopped and laughed. 'It happens.' Then looking around brightly, 'I notice you have an organ in the corner.' She pointed with a long slender hand into a dark recess that harboured an old upright piano next to a ferocious looking amplifier.

'Do you play? Maybe I can hear some later – or do I have to wait for a special night?'

'No. I can't play it. My wife is more of the entertainer but, as I said, she's away at the moment.'

He stopped for a second. 'But if you can play, then please, be my guest,' and he swept his hand in a wide gesture towards the corner.

She laughed. 'Did I tell you that my name is Caroline? Well, I can't play the piano, but I don't mind a bit of a singsong.'

Roy stopped, surprised, looking at her for a second, forgetting to smile. If she liked a bit of a singsong, then he was the Pope. Roy was still prepared to hedge against his instincts, to give her the benefit of the doubt, putting the odd feelings he had about her down simply to his personal charisma – but whatever it was she was after, she would be single minded about it.

'So, you like a singsong. Well, you've come to the right place, darling.'

Roy decided she was now definitely taking the mickey, and he went off down the bar to serve some customers, not in a huff but to give himself time to think; wondering if he should be put out by her. But it seemed too light and easy for that although she was still definitely sending him up – but in a very nice way, he finally decided, so that was okay. Roy normally hated being teased, especially by women. It made him feel small under their gaze.

When he came back a few minutes later, Caroline had returned to the magazine. At his approach, she looked up, smiling brightly, tapping her finger on a page.

'Well, whoever turns this little parish number out is a great loss to Fleet Street, I must say. It gives the word 'parochialism' new depths. There's a story here about someone's mother. It goes on for two or three columns with absolutely no point to it – or didn't until I noticed a large advert for her son's bar immediately opposite. I guess that's the point. The advert!'

Roy smiled. 'I suppose so. But it's pretty harmless. You buy a block advert and you get your mother a mention and the man who turns it out makes a living.'

Caroline paused for a second. 'It's a moot point. Which came first - the advert or the article. But thinking about it, they probably come together like the animals in Noah's ark. Can I have another spritzer, please?'

Roy filled her glass. He was trying to eavesdrop on a discussion further down the bar. It seemed to be about the price of drinks in other bars. To his surprise Caroline nodded.

'I had a girl friend, Emma Mallory, who used to work on one of those science magazines. In fact, she was one of those girls who always knew more than was good for them, and she always said…'

But Roy, a bottle poised unpoured above the glass, interrupted her. 'Did you say Emma Mallory?'

'Why? Do you know her?' Caroline looked up, her eyes widening only slightly in surprise.

Roy returned her gaze for a full five seconds before answering.

'Well, if it's the same person. I used to go out with an Emma Milford. One smart lady. Came from a good family – or so she said. Never got to meet them. I met her at a party in Chelsea. A bit of a nutter, though. Tallish, not bad looking. Always had a monocle. This must have been ten years ago. Is it the same one?'

As he finished, Roy was genuinely animated for the first time. Caroline was nodding vigorously.

'It certainly sounds like her.' She paused. 'The one I knew always had a monocle too. Must be the same one, not too many people wear monocles!' she paused for a second. 'Have you seen her recently? - Maybe you've a photo of her?' She was studying him, eyes wide open, frank and earnest.

Roy hesitated for a heartbeat. 'Yes. Upstairs. I have one upstairs, I think. I'll get it in a minute.'

He finished making the spritzer and after attending to several other orders, with a quick glance round, locked the till and disappeared through the curtained door behind the bar.

When he returned, he was carrying a yellow folder. Putting it down on the bar and ignoring a particular clamour from the far end of the counter, he began carefully to leaf through a sheaf of coloured prints. Eventually, selecting one, he handed it to her.

Caroline studied it for a few seconds, moving it under the light and furrowing her brow. 'Yes, that's her. My old friend Emma.'

She placed it back on the bar, directly between them, saying, 'Well, it's a small world and no mistake. Of all the bars I could have walked into, I walk into yours. You're Emma's ex! She never mentioned you. But then she never did talk much about her private life.'

As she spoke, Caroline was carefully rotating the photo with a long forefinger. They both studied it in silence for a few more seconds before tapping it gently, she announced.

'It was taken here surely? It's a beach scene. In Spain isn't it? But I thought you knew her from London?'

Roy was silent for a moment, then said very casually: 'That's what it looks like, but it wasn't taken here. It was somewhere else. I think it was the only photo she had on her. I remember us laughing because she said she'd borrowed her sister's bikini and it was too tight – you can see that.' It was Roy's turn to tap the photograph.

'I didn't know she had a sister,' interrupted Caroline.

'Oh, perhaps I got it wrong,' said Roy. 'It was a long time ago.'

'Well, whatever.' said Caroline. 'She hasn't changed much. And as I said, she wasn't one to give away much about her private life, was she?'

It was plainly a rhetorical question. Lifting her glass, she took a long sip.

'Well, I'll drink to that,' Roy answered, raising a glass he kept permanently filled below the counter. Things were beginning to take on more definition. They clinked glasses, exchanging tight smiles.

Behind the smile, Caroline had already moved on, focussing on the thorny path ahead of her, wondering how often Roy washed, things like that and so the night went on.

She stayed in plain view on a stool directly opposite his little work-station where he made the drinks. Her vigil was unnecessary. No other women showed any interest in Roy; not for himself, that is, although he quite plainly was the centre of interest as Roy, owner and server of drinks at the Winking Frog… the Blinking Frog.

A weary inevitability suffused her - it would just have to be called something like that, she thought. She'd got her first clear intimation of the uphill nature of the job at hand on hearing the name of the bar for the first time.

At 3am, Roy turned the big, black, state-of-the-art, circa 1995, amplifier down a decibel or two. By half-past-three, things started to wind down. Just before four, he went outside to stack and chained up the two tables and six chairs that furnished an outdoor terrace. They were retained precariously on a narrow, garbage strewn strip of pavement, their real purpose a reference point, a locator for the bar – no one ever sat there except passing drunks lurching home from other bars.

Prompt on four he dragged the main street door shut, explaining at large that it was already well past the official closing time.

Caroline was again enveloped in stillness, hardly moving except to occasionally lift her spritzer. But on hearing Roy shouting last orders, she came to life and asked loudly for one last drink before relapsing back into silence, only moving her head to follow Roy as he jollied resisting knots of customers from the bar.

These last residues of exhausted parties were finally ushered out into the street through a fire door leading off to one side, Roy assuring them loudly, as they stumbled off into the warm dark night, that he would see them all again tomorrow night.

By then, Roy and Caroline had reached a silent understanding; words had become too specific to risk. They both knew what was going to happen if things were left to themselves. That was certainly Roy's reading of it. He didn't ask himself why such a smart young woman would want to make such an obvious play for him. Such questions simply never occurred to him, despite it happening less and less.

It was no mystery. She was simply on holiday – and being on holiday meant doing things you would not do at home. And anyway, she had to wait. She'd told him several times of an arrangement to meet her cousin here at the Winking Frog, that he had the only key to their rented apartment or whatever. Roy had not really listened to the detail; with him, most conversation involving third parties became aural wallpaper.

And the cousin hadn't shown up and she'd not seemed too put out by this, there hadn't been a big thing about going off to look for him or anything. Roy missed nothing in his little bar. It was old habits from the street, he told himself. He had a nose for it, for unlikely behaviour, behaviour that was outside its context.

Finally, closing the door on the last reluctant customer, he turned back to Caroline, saying, 'You'd think these people hadn't got hotels to go to.' It was something he always said at that moment, even when alone. Then coming up behind her, he wordlessly slipped his arms around her.

Caroline immediately responded by tilting her head back and they began to kiss. Roy's whole approach was matter of fact, a long practised and calculated technique; he hardly needed to think about it, its familiarity and lack of surprise carrying its own authority. And it often worked.

The kissing had already gone on too long for Caroline; kissing was anyway too intimate, too special for such an engineered encounter. Twisting towards him, she slipped off the stool and taking Roy by the hand, led him round the bar and towards the door in the back wall of the bar, asking, 'This way?' as she opened it.

He nodded back, silent, a little put out that she had taken the initiative so early and so easily. Modern girls! He thought. After all, he was the one supposed to be making the moves.

Then he realised that this must mean she didn't need much warming up, another plus. Up narrow stairs they went, Caroline still pushing ahead and occasionally smiling back over her shoulder. The stairs took a half turn and at the top was a narrow passage. The first door they came to was open and Roy found his voice, 'In there.' To his annoyance it came out scratchy and uncertain.

Ahead on the floor, Caroline saw a fusty unmade bed. By a dark wall, a heavily shaded lamp threw a dull yellow glimmer down its near side, catching and highlighting greyish, crumpled sheets. The rest of the room remained resolutely in a deep gloom. The lamp's base was an old champagne bottle and the shade was round and brown and decorated with champagne labels. This alone made Caroline shudder internally.

Beyond the circle of dull yellow light, she made out the front of an open clothes rack. It ran along the far side of the room, a simple horizontal metal pole running from wall to wall. On it were strung Roy's clothes, but at the far end, for more than half its length, it was empty.

Must be where his Lady Wife's things once hung, she supposed. Then she noticed that the rack was faintly lit from behind. Traces of yellow sodium light leaked in past dark drawn blinds that shrouded an unseen window.

'How nice,' said Caroline, much too brightly. 'I see your wife took her clothes when she left. Well, no doubt they were no use to you. You didn't want to wear them, did you?' She added.

In the half dark, her broad smile, lit from below, had become a leer.

Roy realised two things simultaneously. This girl was fast on the uptake and she was definitely out to take the piss. Silently, he pushed her towards the bed. There was always one way of shutting them up. Seconds later he was inside her and by the time she had managed to detach her knickers from where they'd clung to her right foot, he had finished and was getting off. Well at least it was quick.

'Where can I wash?' was all she said.

He pointed towards the open doorway. 'Second on the left. You'll see it. Next to the toilet.'

She looked up at him. Against the light from the doorway, the dark hair on his arms stood out as clear as the whiskers in a Rembrandt self-portrait.

'I have to get to sleep now. I have to be up in five hours. I've a beer delivery coming,' and stepping over her, with no more ceremony, he lay down and turned towards the wall.

CHAPTER THREE

A couple of hours later Caroline was furtively crouched over the telephone on the floor in the front room of the apartment. Her plan had been to feign sleep while resolutely staying awake, but Roy's snoring had made it no contest. Now, half blinded by the dust flecked early morning sunlight streaming through a lopsided, broken lattice blind, she knelt listening to the voice mail being played back. She was looking for one particular message. The trouble was there were no messages – nothing but an automated recording tirelessly telling her in Spanish that there were no messages.

Finding it impossible to maintain the awkward crouch for long, she straightened up to survey the room. She was wondering what to do next. She was after a particular telephone number, a contact number for Emma in England. It could be anywhere, on a voice mail message, in a book or scrawled on the wall, but she was sure it would be somewhere in that room.

Suddenly, the phone rang. It was ear splitting in the heavy morning silence of the small apartment. Without thinking, only wanting to stop it, Caroline snatched up the receiver, mouthing 'Hello' in a whisper. There was no answer, only silence at the other end. But not the silence of a non connection or a faltering international call, but the more sinister silence of an open, live line, of the restrained presence of someone on the other end. To Caroline it was almost palpable.

Still without thinking, she repeated, 'Hello. Hello. Who is it? Hello,' more loudly this time and as instantly, could have kicked herself. A few more seconds of charged silence elapsed and then there came the unmistakable effect of a receiver being dropped back onto its cradle – not quietly replaced, but dropped. Immediately, her ear was filled with a dial tone so loud it deafened her.

Rocking back onto her heels, she stared down at the telephone. This could just have been a major, major mistake, answering the call, actually speaking. After a few more seconds staring at the silent phone, she shook herself and glanced at her watch. It was seven-thirty in the morning.

Who on earth would call the owner of a Spanish tourist bar at such an hour? Certainly, nobody who was at all acquainted with their killing routines. Maybe it was a wrong number or a long-distance call; a call from another time zone. Several time zones and the caller had got the local time in Spain wrong, added instead of subtracting the time difference. It couldn't have been Roy's wife. Caroline was sure of that, because she would have said something. So, of interested parties – callers with the capacity to cause problems – it only left Emma.

She looked down, studying her hands, running over the incident again, until the vivid light streaming through the blind finally brought her back to where she was again. If it had been Emma, she'd wait and then call again and maybe next time Caroline wouldn't be there and Roy would take the call. This must not happen, she thought. A new worry then intruded. Maybe, the caller had recognised her – it could be enough that a woman had answered! And if it had been Emma calling, she'd know it was her, for sure. This was now the wild card.

Caroline remained in her awkward semi-crouch over the telephone, the aching muscles now forgotten. Deep in thought, it was a few moments before she became aware that the balance of the room had subtly and silently altered – maybe the light patterns. Whatever it was, something had changed and changed quite recently. Caroline turned slowly round. Roy was standing watching her, motionless, from the doorway.

She got to her feet slowly, taking her time, trying not to panic as she sought to remember her cover story she'd so carefully fabricated.

'Couldn't sleep, so came out here and saw the phone and remembered I have to call my cousin. He'll be wondering where I got to, as I didn't come home last night.'

Caroline trailed off. Then forcing a smile. 'Anyway, I'd better go. Don't want my cousin coming looking for me. He's a bit deranged, especially in the morning before he's had a chance to have a drink,' and she tapped her head significantly as she moved passed Roy to the door and pulled it open.

He watched her go. She had timed it perfectly and he did not try to stop her, still plainly not up to speed on what was going on. Then after a few seconds he came to himself and hurried after her, along the passage and down the stairs, even pushing ahead to let her out the back door onto the vacant land behind.

Once outside in the bright morning sunshine, she started to breathe easier again. For a minute it could have gone either way, she thought – and with her 'cousin' unavailable. Reaching open ground, she turned away from the bright sunlight to face Roy. He had stopped in the shadow of the doorway.

'So, it looks as if your wife doesn't have any plans to come back in the near future.'

She cocked an eyebrow as she spoke. This seemed to provoke Roy.

'What's it got to do with you anyway? He shot back. You don't know her. You only turned up for a fuck.'

'So elegantly put. You have obviously such a way with words.'

She gave a wintry little smile before continuing.

'But it also could have plenty to do with me – and my cousin.' And seeing the sudden alarm race across his face, realising she'd gone too far, added: 'No man is an island. That's all I meant. See you.'

And with a last impertinent little moue, Caroline was gone.

CHAPTER FOUR

In a flat in Holland Park, London, Emma dropped the phone back on to its cradle and sat staring at it, as if she'd just discovered it was covered in plague virus. So, they'd found Roy already, her long fingers pulling in agitation at the waist band of her pyjamas.

She'd woken earlier from a fitful sleep with the sudden realisation that she'd allowed too much time to go by since her last call to Roy. Getting no answer then, she'd stupidly left him a message and now four days later Caroline was ensconced and answering his phone. But how had they found Roy so quickly? They were not the police. Roy must have helped them, maybe inadvertently. He wasn't bright. God knows – it was one of his few virtues.

But then another virtue had been that he knew the rules – unwritten of course, and a compelling enough reason at the time to use him.

'But I also know the rules,' she thought wryly, 'and number one was you don't tell people things they don't need to know' – and in Roy's case, would never need to know. So, how come Felix had connected the two of them so quickly? And of course, it would be Felix because Caroline was still inclined to think in straight lines, like a law abiding citizen. Emma was sure she'd never mentioned Roy to them or anyone else, for that matter, and she was also quite certain that she'd left no record of his existence in the house in the Lake District.

As she thought about it, she relaxed a little. So what if they'd found Roy? All was not lost. He knew very little and nothing at all about their money stashed in the bank down there. She'd told him it was still in England and was, as far as he knew, the reason she'd gone back to London. He'd no idea the money was anywhere but where she'd said it was, in the house in the Lake District. That was what she had led Roy to believe – and even if he didn't, it was all he knew.

Emma had kept him in a box, like everyone else she dealt with, on a 'need to know basis', as she would have put it. She saw it the same as programming a washing machine. You didn't tell it your life story; you punched its wash cycle buttons.

But Caroline's, and very probably Felix's, arrival on the scene, must have come via Roy. That was for sure. Yet how had they found Roy? Then she remembered that he had her phone number to the house in the Lake District. He'd told her he'd lost it – and maybe he had, but she'd written it out on a piece of paper and left it for him, so it had existed somewhere in that unwholesome little bar. She'd given it to him the first time they'd met, even before she'd appreciated that he might have a wider usefulness. It now looked all a bit gratuitous.

But surely he hadn't used it. Surely he hadn't phoned her there! When she'd called to give him her new number in London - a pay-as-you go mobile number actually – she'd specifically told him never to use that old Lake District number. She remembered that she'd been quite emphatic – mentioned that there were some very disgruntled people there; that he'd be inviting trouble if he ever used it, maybe an early demise, most likely preceded by some form of artistic dismemberment.

And now Caroline was answering his phone in Spain. It had been Caroline; no one else. Of this Emma was certain. You don't know someone for over two years, live cheek to jowl with them for all that time and then get confused about their voice, no matter how far away or brief and tinny it may have come across.

So, how had they connected her to Roy? They wouldn't be able to trace her call just now; she'd used a prefix code to conceal the number. But the question remained, how had they got on to Roy so quickly? And if he chose to talk, what could he actually tell them – that they'd had rapid and unnuanced sex a few times and that she'd mentioned she'd come into a lot of money which hadn't been strictly kosher and that she wanted him to help her get it out of the United Kingdom and into Spain.

All he had was their number in the Lake District and a number for a museum call box in Exhibition Row. They would probably have guessed that she was in London anyway, but that was as useful as knowing which haystack the needle was in.

What Roy also had, although he didn't know it - and never would, she fervently hoped, shuddering at her own stupidity – was the key to a safe deposit box containing upwards of four million dollars. She had hidden it the bedroom of his shabby little bar, stuck out of sight in a line of exposed brickwork immediately behind the bed. Her plan had been, when she got back, to get Roy out of the way while she recovered it.

Glancing at the clock, she saw it was seven in the morning, eight in Spain. Too early to do anything, she lit a cigarette and sitting down on a kitchen chair, stared at the smoke as it spiralled up towards an extractor fan.

Leaving any message on his answering machine, she now knew, had been a very stupid thing to do. There was no way of saying who would eventually listen to it and although it had not been in plain language – she hadn't actually said: "Come to England and help me get all the money I've stolen, back to Spain for me," but she had couched it in such arch and stagy coding that it's very artfulness cried out the clandestine.

Emma tried to calm herself by going over the whole business carefully once again. As far as she knew, Roy lived on his own. He had mentioned a wife in the usual disparaging tones that such men always use, but as Emma had not seen any wife or any signs of her in the bar or, more significantly, in the sordid little bedroom in which he apparently passed the other half of his mundane existence, she had come to believe there wasn't an active Mrs Roy around anymore.

She also knew that it was a mistake to take anything that men said on trust, especially in such circumstances. But he'd been so enthusiastic about her staying with him, hanging out at the Winking Frog, that she'd believed him, a conviction reinforced by being unable to see any earthly reason why another woman would linger there without an equally pressing inducement.

She shuddered again. She had accepted his word simply because she could see no reason not to – intellectual laziness amounting to carelessness, and she was the one who always went on about genius being 100% about detail.

But wife or no wife, why hadn't she heard back from him? There was something going on there. The more Emma thought about it, the more she began to think that maybe her touch had begun to desert her. At best, Roy was a cheap little smudger and she'd offered him the best deal ever likely to grace his entire, accident prone, recidivistic life – and yet he'd not even returned her call.

Stubbing her cigarette out, she decided there and then to go to Spain as soon as possible, to discover what was going on and also to remove the safe key, herself and the money from his life forever.

She'd stupidly piled miscalculation on miscalculation. After successfully 'acquiring' the money and getting it safely out of England, she'd quite gratuitously jeopardised everything with a hideously complicated final act by moving in with an unwashed and repulsive little cretin and then, to make matters even worse, leaving the safe deposit key hidden in the brickwork immediately behind his permanently unmade, mouldy bed while she returned to England to pick up her beloved dog.

At least, she bitterly congratulated herself, she hadn't attached a tag to it saying: "Key to Safety Deposit Box, Benidorm National Bank. Account Number so and so, Secret Password so and so..." Emma was beginning to wonder if she really was the criminal mastermind,she'd privately considered herself to be.

Four hours later, carefully locking the rented flat in Holland Park, she grabbed a cab for Victoria Station and the Gatwick Airport Express. Clarence was sitting proudly beside her on the back seat. A rather stupid although avowedly good natured dog, he'd become the most important thing in her life, after the four million dollars, of course.

Before confirming their tickets, she'd made sure the aircraft's hold, in which Clarence was to travel, was properly pressurised. A kennel was already booked for him on arrival, where he would reside until she had finished her business there.

In the departure lounge with Clarence already safely installed in a dog crate for the flight, Emma carefully looked around, moving to one side, away from the banks of overhead screens and cameras. She considered airports dangerous bottlenecks that could bring to light awkward and unwanted acquaintances without warning.

Impatiently plucking at the long leather strap of her handbag, she debated the plan ahead. Emma sometimes thought that she had chosen her path in life because it required the wholesale manipulation of her fellow men, and here she almost literally meant men. Although her powers over them were extensive and potent she could do very little with women; they seemed mostly immune to even her most subtle set pieces.

This train of thought soon broadened into a consideration of her own life. She often wished she could be more interested in other people, both men and women, but she'd long known that she was actually much more interested in herself and the small stage centred on her. It was a setting she frequently felt the need to revive with gratuitous interventions.

Maybe, when it was all over and she was safely away with the money, she'd go into therapy. She needed to know what was behind this urge to introduce unnecessary risk, to always lift the beat, go the extra yard – because this project, which until now had gone so seamlessly, was now juddering to a halt on the back of this unnecessary diversion to Roy's bedroom, introduced, she had to suppose, purely to relieve boredom. She was like the artist who could never finish a painting, one more brush stroke and the chimera of perfection would be achieved – and now 'they' were down there in the awkward shape of Caroline; and where Caroline was, Felix would not be far away.

Emma crossed to a stall set on large yellow cart wheels made up like a twenties hot dog stand, to buy a bottle of still water. And that's another mystery, she wryly thought, because for someone who desires more and more money, my tastes are simple, almost austere.

Back in her seat, she reflected again on the presence of Caroline in Spain. Roy was such a pushover that it would take her less than one evening to have got into his greasy little bed and into his confidence. Emma sighed, grateful for the abrupt interruption brought by her flight being called.

CHAPTER FIVE

The Winking Frog, across from the beach, skulked amidst a row of bars, fast food joints, boutiques, mini supermarkets, car hire agencies - all, at first glance, as distinguishable from each other as the teeth on a plastic comb. On the other side, the beach was a strip of sand about seventy metres wide where Spain ran out into the deep blue Mediterranean, which on that day, as on most days, was a lifting, sliding swell of glassy chemicals.

Emma sat in a deck chair close to the road and diagonally opposite the bar. She was in a black bikini that highlighted the blanched whiteness of her skin, topped with a large black sun hat with a deep brim concealing everything under it, including her expensive black sunglasses. She sat with her back to the sea, content in her unobtrusiveness as yet another tourist.

She was watching the bar. It was about midday and it hadn't opened yet. She'd already seen Roy come out and stand staring up and down the road. There was a note of impatience about his stance and she concluded that a beer delivery was late. She was unafraid that he would see her because she was enough of a psychologist to know that the beach and its human furniture were all but indiscernible to him.

She also knew with Roy that it was personal, having told her one drunken evening that he actually hated the beach and had not been on it for years, seeing it as the author of all his misfortunes, of his slavery to the Winking Frog and the treadmill of the tourist trade.

Caroline came out to join him, looking up and down the street. Emma lifted a magazine to her face. Caroline was different. She had eyes that could see. She would not be invisible to her.

About an hour later, Roy left the bar, neither looking left or right. He was alone and there was a purpose to his stride. This meant that Caroline was still inside so maybe she was here to stay – or at least until she got what she'd come for. Roy was carrying some letters and Emma surmised that he was probably going to the post office in the commercial part of the town.

Getting to her feet and pulling a wrap around her, she was smiling inwardly, thinking about there being a 'commercial' part to a town where already every square metre was devoted to it. She asked an English family sunbathing nearby to watch her things, a towel and a magazine, and then set off to follow Roy, keeping to the beach until she was obliged to cross the road to trail him up a side street and away from the sea.

Emma shadowed him to the post office where he faithfully posted the letters. The post office was not the place to talk, she decided, it was far too public – too many expats hanging around their post boxes, exchanging tales of the latest bureaucratic impediments to life in paradise.

Instead, she waited until he'd paid a quick visit to a Quiksave Supermarket festooned with posters claiming to supply 'EVERYTHING AS SOLD AT

HOME' and had then sought out a shaded corner on the terrace of a nearby bar – a bar, Emma noticed, that seemed unique in that it was owned by a Spaniard. Only then did she feel it safe to approach him.

Giving him a few seconds grace, she entered from a side door, the dark interior welcoming her in. Still unnoticed, she got herself a beer at the bar and took it over to where Roy sat, facing the street. She came up quickly from behind and sat down directly across the table from him, her back to the street. Engrossed in his mail, he eventually looked up, surprise changing to alarm when he recognised her through her dark disguise.

'Hello Darling.' Emma began. 'You *are* a quick worker. I see I've already been replaced in your affections. My, but you do get through us poor girls. Has she offered to wash your socks yet?'

Roy shut his mouth slowly, eyes flickering like the lights in a pin ball machine, trying to catch up with the implications of Emma's sudden appearance.

Finally, he managed, 'What do you want?' It came out harsh and strained.

'What a nice welcome from my old lover. I was frankly expecting something warmer.'

Emma paused for a long second.

'I was also expecting a reply to my message - or are you now so rich that you can turn down offers of hundreds of thousands of pounds?'

She instantly regretted using the plural. It definitely sent the wrong signal.

Roy didn't answer, still trying to grasp the significance of her arrival, finally he said, 'What are you talking about? What message? I didn't get any fucking message. What was it - an email or something?'

Emma realised he was genuinely puzzled. Relaxing back in her chair, she took a long sip at her beer, sighing inwardly. It had been too hot on the beach and now it looked like any conversation with him would be built from bricks without straw.

'I sent you a coded message as agreed. About four days ago, to come to England and meet me for you know what. I left a message on your answering machine. Surely, you must have got it?' She arched an eyebrow, waiting.

Roy continued to stare at her for a few more seconds before turning back to his drink. When he looked up, his face had tightened.

'I got no message. In fact, I haven't had a message from anyone for days. In fact, as far as no messages go, there seems to be a lot going on that I don't know about.'

As he finished speaking he sat back, sullen and defensive.

Emma looked at him and then looked away. It hadn't crossed her mind that he might not actually have received her message. When she turned back to him, he was still staring into his beer.

'It was definitely the right number,' she continued. 'It was your voice and the number was the same. I suppose there was some little tart there who listened to it and then wiped it. I would have thought that with a deal like ours coming off, you'd have kept your mind on business for a few days.'

She paused to take a mouthful of beer, her eyes never leaving him. 'Who could have got my message then? Although it doesn't really matter as it wouldn't have meant much to anyone else. I didn't say anything specific. I didn't go into details.'

Roy didn't answer right away, instead he sat back to consider this latest piece of information. Then speaking slowly as if finding his way around a difficult thought, he said:

'It must have been Rita.' He paused again, 'My wife. She was here a few days ago to pick up her things. Yes, and then deleted the message. It could only have been her. She must have thought it was from a girlfriend.'

'Your wife?' It was Emma's turn to be surprised. 'I didn't know you had a wife. You never mentioned a wife before.' Emma was genuinely surprised. 'In fact, I remember you specifically said you didn't have a wife. So where did she spring from?'

Emma stopped speaking for a second and looked him over.

'When I was here before, you never mentioned her,' she sighed. 'You told me you lived alone. But of course, you wouldn't tell me in case it meant you wouldn't get me into bed. That's it. You were pretending to be single and all the time there was a wife in the background. How stupid of me. Of course, you'd be married. Where else would you have got the stake to start your own bar? I missed that, didn't I?'

Emma put it as a rhetorical question. She was busy mentally back peddling through the past scenario, seeing how this might change things. Then she relaxed. Not much really, she concluded. It didn't matter. She'd be finished with Roy once she'd recovered the safe deposit key – and in any case she'd only picked on him for somewhere discreet to stay to avoid signing in to a hotel. He could have ten wives for all she cared, once she had the key back again - but now it meant getting Caroline off the premises as well. That would be a final job for Roy. She smiled at him.

Roy was managing to look both truculent and sheepish at the same time. Emma thought it suited him. Deciding it was time to start spinning a little bit of the ephemeral, she turned her eyes to the floor and leaning in towards him, began to speak slowly and confidentially.

'I mentioned my place in the Lake District – gave you the number. Then I sent you my London number – in the message you didn't get. I wanted you to go to the Lake District to collect my money. It's hidden there. I'll tell you about that later.'

Emphasising 'money', she looked him full in the face. He was shaking his head.

'Well, anyway,' Emma continued, 'you'll have to go there as soon as possible. Close up the bar and go and collect my money.'

Roy was shaking his head. 'And what are you going to do while I risk my fucking neck getting your money. You're leaving me to take all the risks!'

'You must be joking. You think I'm going to disappear when there's millions of dollars at stake. Don't worry. I'll be right here waiting. After all, you have to come back here whatever, haven't you? I mean, you're not going to walk away from all this hard earned equity.'

She almost laughed out loud as an expression of low cunning which, despite his best efforts, had now colonised his face.

'Of course, I've got to come back,' he broke in. 'It's in my name and since Rita's done a runner, she doesn't deserve to get a fucking penny.'

Emma registered the name, Rita. 'Well, whatever! You've got to get a move on as it's more complicated than that. There are other people at the old house in the Lake District. In fact, the people I took the money from are there. Except for Caroline, that is, who is at this moment waiting in your bed for you. Maybe waiting for the phone to ring, but definitely keeping an eye on you for a start. That's why she's here. You realise that? You're their contact to me, their only one.' Emma stopped to let it sink in.

Roy's face drained of colour. Christ, thought Emma, I should have introduced them more subtly, more gradually.

'Caroline – you know Caroline? She's in the bar! How do you know she's in the bar? How do you know her?' Roy stopped speaking as further implications dawned on him.

'Unlike you, I don't walk about with my eyes closed,' retorted Emma. 'That's Caroline, my ex partner, out here! No doubt to recover the money. For some reason they're convinced it belongs to them. And they've found you already, haven't they. It's lucky you don't know more or you could be dangerous – for them,' Emma added hastily.

'What's she doing here? And believe me it's not entirely because she can't resist your body. Maybe she's waiting for the phone to ring, do you think?' She leant back in her chair, studying the impact of her words.

Roy was glaring at Emma, his face slowly returning to normal.

'She's not waiting for the phone to ring, I can tell you that, because for some reason, it got cut off a couple of days ago...' then he trailed off again as the implications of what Emma had just said sank in.

Still putting it together, he continued: 'Are you saying that Caroline is not here by accident. That she's not here on holiday like she said?'

Now the expression on his face was a delight with the dawning realisation that yet another smart woman had been playing him like a fish in a bucket.

Emma shook her head, still smiling.

'She's here looking for me,' she said. 'They know about us. That's how she found you. When I hid the money and took off, I called you here. They must have traced the call somehow. She's here waiting for me to contact you. She's here because she knows I hid the money somewhere in England before getting out. She's here to find me through you – by staying close to you…'

'Oh, I see!' Emma said laughing out loud. 'You'd put it all down to your irresistible charm – Caroline suddenly flinging herself at you. Poor Roy! I think that by the time this is all over, you may be a little wiser as well as richer, of course.' She added hastily.

There was another long silence and Emma decided that she'd maybe said too much. It was time to listen, to see how Roy was taking it. Eventually, he broke the silence.

'Do you think they have Rita? Maybe she went to your house, wherever it is, the one in the Lake District, and they've got her and she's told them all.'

'But I thought you said she didn't know anything. She didn't know about the money. That you'd told her nothing,' Emma cut in, suddenly alarmed. 'How would she even know where to go?

She's not likely to end up at the house in the Lake District on a shopping trip to Tooting Bec is she?'

Emma stopped, appraising him, trying to work out what might have happened from her knowledge of the man.

'You'd better make up your mind what your wife knows, because it could be serious. It's too late to worry about saving face now. Maybe you hinted about our little deal, said enough for her to put two and two together.'

Emma paused while they both thought about this. 'If you did, we're both in big trouble.' As she finished, she wished she hadn't said that. It might predispose him to lie to her more.

'What I mean,' she hurried on, 'is that now you must tell me exactly what you told her. It's too late for blame or anything like that. This could be a damage limitation exercise now.'

Roy shook his head violently. 'I never told her anything. She doesn't know a thing. Yea, as if I'd be likely to tell her and then she'd be in for half and I'd never be shot of her. Anyway, now that you mention it, how much am I in for then?'

Roy finished strongly, coming back off the canvas, glaring at her, trying to wrest the initiative. He was thinking that she'd soon have plenty of time to realise she had been patronising the wrong man. Then, like Emma a few moments before, he realised that he mustn't give too much away. This was no air head bimbo he was dealing with. It would be a good move to put on a show of good faith by haggling over his share, as if he really intended to return to Spain with it all.

'What about fifty-fifty then?' He suddenly demanded. 'You don't think I'm going to take all these risks if your friends are on to me! And they're pretty heavy, by the sound of it – for a measly hundred thousand. It's not nearly enough. I'm the one who has everything to lose. And it also looks as if I'm the only one you can trust. The only one you've got.' He was almost cheerful when he finished.

'I'll give you forty percent and that's final,' Emma said, almost absently and after hardly a pause, her thoughts still on Rita and what she might know. Whatever it was, it had probably not come directly from Roy. His reply about not intending to give Rita a penny had been entirely convincing. She brought herself back to the present.

'But I don't want any more renegotiations after this. That's it. I really hate people who agree to something and then try to boost it up later. Have you ever heard of the parable of the vineyard – never mind, but you should look it up one day. It's a good read.' She closed with a frosty little smile.

There was a long pause as each got on with their private thoughts, before Roy broke in again.

'So, what do I do now? I can't just go back and close the bar and take off. Caroline – if she's here to keep an eye on me – is bound to want to know where I'm going, closing up in the middle of the season like that. People will think I'm crazy.'

'It's not the middle of the season yet,' Emma pointed out, 'and you can tell people that you're going to try to get your wife to come back. It'll do your reputation no end of good. Make you look like a human being.

'And as far as Caroline's concerned," Emma added, 'it'll be what she wants to hear. Just confess all to her. Put your hand on your heart and lie. You shouldn't find that too difficult. After all, you've told me enough already and I've only known you a few weeks. Tell her that you got a letter from a friend saying your wife is starting legal proceeding to take the bar and that you have to go to England right away and that she can stay in the bar until you come back.'

'She knows who you are anyway,' Roy interrupted. 'She talked about you. It came up in conversation that we both know you and she asked if I had a photo of you. I showed her that old one you left here. I didn't tell her I'd seen you recently. I pretended we'd met back in London when you were at college. Didn't want to tell her anything I didn't need to.' He stopped, as if waiting to be patted like a dog.

'So, your paranoia came in useful after all and she established that I was who I am, eh? Very clever! And if you imagine it came up by accident you also believe that the Pope's not a Catholic.'

Emma paused for a second to think. 'It's my guess that she'll make some excuse to go with you or at least be on the same plane. Remember, as far as you're concerned, she's just a summer love and that she knows nothing about our business.

'And where do I pick up the money?' Roy asked. 'Is it in some safe deposit or something? I don't want any trouble with them watching me now.

'This is the tricky bit.' Emma put on a serious face. 'The money's hidden near my house in the Lake District. It's my house even though the rest of the gang will be there waiting for me, so you will have to be clever about it. I'll explain it all someday, but suffice to say, I was doing a bit of business with them and they tried to rip me off. But it's a long story – and don't worry about finding the money. I'll give you exact directions. It won't be difficult to get at; it's in a shed in the grounds of my house.'

Emma stopped and took a folded sheet of paper out of her beach bag and flattened it out on the table.

'I'm not going to give you this so you have to commit it to memory now. It's not complicated. You'll see a shed, a sort of summerhouse with a yellow door. It's in the garden and it's never locked.'

Emma started sketching away, drawing a block for the house and a smaller one near it for the shed. A rough circle round everything indicated the boundary wall to the property. Emma drew in some trees, taking time over their detail. She'd been to art school.

'Inside there's a lot of gardening junk, wheelbarrows and a lawn mower. The lawn mower is all in pieces in one corner, the engine parts lying about behind it on an old bag, a jute bag. Get the bag by its corners and pull it towards you - the place is so full of stuff there's only one clear bit of floor to stand on. It'll move okay. I arranged it.

'Under the bag it looks just like the square panels of a wooden floor. It's actually a trap door. Use a screwdriver or something and prise it up. It should come up easily. Below it is a shallow hole, and in it are several black plastic bin bags with the money. My money. Take it and go. Okay?'

She was looking at him. He was nodding. 'And when you come to take the money, make sure that you don't have to go back to the house for anything. Be ready to leave.'

She looked at him again. He was still nodding.

Emma took the paper and folded it carefully and put it back in her bag.

'You can't miss it,' she reassured him. 'It's the only shed in the garden and it's got a yellow door.'

She smiled at him encouraging. A smile that said they were a team, that they were equals.

'When do you want me to go? It sounds as if the sooner it's done the better, eh?'

'Go tomorrow. Here's five hundred euros. On the way back to the bar stop in at that travel place and get yourself a ticket to London. Caroline's going to go back to England anyway, so act naturally, as if you had nothing to hide, as if you're above suspicion. She'll follow you and you can bet she'll have someone on the aeroplane, if she is not on it herself. Be quite open and natural with her. She's street smart so don't try to kid her. Okay.'

Emma studied Roy in silence for a few seconds. 'Caroline will offer to take you back to the house in the Lake District, and once there, you can sneak out one night and get the money and go. I don't think I'm going to stay here while you're gone – in this awful little town, I mean.'

'And anyway,' she continued, 'you'd better not come straight back here. It's the first place they'll come looking for you. Later you might have to handle questions from them. That could be, let us say, the down side of our little transaction, but that's why I've agreed to pay you so very well for such a simple little job!' Emma added hurriedly, knowing how prickly he was.

They sat for another ten minutes or so while Roy, now suddenly animated by the prospect of so much money, insisted on going over it again, step by step. Emma described once again where the money was hidden, rehearsing him patiently on how to silently open the floor panel and telling him again how the money would be immediately below and to make sure he closed the panel again and the door to the hut as well. She warned him not to swing the beam of the torch about and emphasised how important it was to leave everything in place – exactly how he'd found it.

She showed him the map once again. It was actually a map of the entrance to the secret drugs laboratory. She also failed to mention that there were about twenty thousand pounds worth of invisible intruder alarms monitoring the whole area. Roy wouldn't get within five yards of the yellow door to the shed without being discovered.

Smiling encouragingly as they parted, Emma gave him an affectionate little peck on the cheek. 'And if Caroline discovers that she's got to return home suddenly, as well, offer to get her a ticket on the same flight. Girls like these little touches.'

They parted, Emma staying behind in the little bar until Roy was well clear. Then she made her way carefully back to her deckchair opposite the Winking Frog and took up surveillance again.

Not long after she was back in position, Roy left the bar again, this time in the opposite direction. 'To get their flight tickets,' Emma thought.

Waiting until he was out of sight, she gave him a couple of minutes to come back for something, then getting her mobile phone out and concealing her number, she rang the Winking Frog, knowing that Caroline would answer.

Without giving Caroline a chance to speak, she launched into a breathless discourse:

'Roy, it's Emma. Can't talk long – my mobile's dying on me. I need you here in London ASAP (she spelt it out). Call me the moment you land so we can organise picking up the money. It's in the Lake District – and remember, keep this to yourself. Okay? Byeeee,' and the call was over.

Then gathering her things together, she made her way discreetly along the beach and away from the bar.

CHAPTER SIX

That night it was a Saturday and the bar was very busy. Caroline came in early and made a show of helping out, going unasked behind the bar and washing glasses, keeping abreast of things. She was wearing a black dress, tight and short. Roy decided she was definitely more attractive than Emma. She was also more sympathetic with none of Emma's wry little vitriolic barbs and arrows. He felt more comfortable with Caroline.

He congratulated himself on getting rid of his slut of a wife in time to come into all the money. There would be no return to Spain and the bar afterwards. The bank was welcome to it. It would be a long time before he saw this Godforsaken place again.

At three, as the business slowed and people left for the late bars and discotheques, Roy began to drink seriously. He'd have to make a show for Caroline later, and he needed to be at least halfway high. As the last group of stragglers left, he closed the door behind them and turned back towards her as she was coming out from behind the bar, drying her hands on the dish cloth hanging from her belt.

'I want to go somewhere quiet and have a drink before going to bed,' he said. 'I need to unwind. Let's go to the Garden of Allah. It's a quiet little bar where some of the other bar owners go after they close. It's not far away and we can get a little peace and quiet.'

Caroline nodded and pulled the dishcloth out from her belt and draped it over the stool; she'd got into the part.

Over his shoulder, Roy added, 'I'll be with you in a minute. Just let me put the money away. Bars are a target. Junkies wanting a quick hit break in because they know that any money we've taken is likely to still be on the premises.' He smiled and disappeared up the stairs behind the bar.

Caroline poured herself a weak mixture of white wine and mineral water and waited. She wasn't drunk and she wasn't bored, although she considered that watching a top loading washing machine might have the edge on a night at the Winking Frog.

She'd picked up on Roy's suppressed excitement as soon as he'd come back from his mail run that morning - and being the type of woman, she was, she hadn't waited until he found the right moment to unburden himself. She wasn't even confident that he would, so quite early on in the evening, when he'd been out front in the bar listening to the latest joke from Macclesfield, she'd gone through the pockets of his light linen jacket he'd hung up next to the stereo player. She found a flight ticket for the next afternoon.

Caroline went back to her drink. The call from Emma had been their first tangible lead. It said that even if Emma was still in England, so apparently was the money. Now it would be a case of making it easy for Roy to take her with him.

Laughing inwardly, she rehearsed her response. "Oh how convenient – I'm going back to England myself tomorrow. Where are you going?

To the Lake District? Now there's a coincidence, that's where I'm going. I have a house there. You can stay. Yes, why don't you. I'll drive you there…"

It should be a piece of cake although she still wondered at Emma's judgement, trusting a slippery little dodger like Roy to pick up all that money when everything about him screamed the clandestine – because even if he grew as big as a brontosaurus, he still wouldn't have an honest bone in his body. But that was typical of Emma, as cunning as a snake one moment and the next, pitching everything on the turn of a card.

Or maybe Emma had something really good on Roy. She certainly had a nose for people's weaknesses. It must be that or she was intending to shadow him, but either way, she was taking a huge chance. Now all Caroline had to do was to allow Roy to let his lifeless hair down and tell her all about it, officially.

It didn't take long, Roy's confession and it fitted like the metaphorical silk glove. After finally closing and locking up, they'd gone to the Garden of Allah further down the strip. It was still crowded when they got there but soon began to thin out.

Finding a table right at the back and mercifully away from the main speakers which, despite the lateness of the hour, roared out rock 'n roll through the empty cubits of dark space, they'd settled back with their drinks.

After an awkward silence, Roy suddenly looked over at Caroline saying, 'I have to go to England tomorrow. I've something to do. It means that the bar will be closed.'

'Really! When did you decide this?' Caroline did an accented double take, pretending to be taken aback. 'Has something come up? Did you get a call or something? I hope it's not serious.'

She looked very concerned, which only irritated Roy more. He was having trouble striking the right pose under Caroline's impartial scrutiny. Then smiling demurely, she added. 'Although mine is nothing really serious, I think I had better go back as well. I can always come back later. I quite like it here.'

Roy, obviously somewhat taken aback, answered: 'I'm trying to get a flight for tomorrow afternoon or evening. There are plenty of late flights. I'm going to call them in the morning. Do you want me to ask for a ticket for you as well? They're usually pretty cheap. About sixty pounds one way, but the drawback is we arrive at Gatwick pretty late at night.'

Caroline was nodding. 'That would be okay for me. We can go back together. Where are you going once you get to England?' she asked.

'I've got to do a little job for a friend of mine in the north of England. It'll make me a few bob into the garden.'

'It's nothing criminal is it, Roy?' Caroline laughed provocatively. Then not wanting to go too far, quickly added, '...and why did you say "into the garden" a moment ago? That was strange, does it have something to do with a garden? Or don't you mean, "into the bargain?"'

Roy looked at her as if she had sprouted velvet antlers.

'What are you fucking talking about... for the love of Christ. I never said "into the garden." Sometimes I think you're short of a marble or two. And No! It's not criminal and I stand to make a few bob.'

'How much?' Caroline asked casually. She was actually preoccupied with something else. When she looked up, Roy was tapping his nose. Despite the strain, Caroline nearly burst out laughing. It was so utterly burlesque.

'That's for me to know and you to find out,' he finally said.

She sat back into her chair and took a long sip of beer. It was too good, just too good. Someone like Roy didn't tell virtual strangers such things, she thought, not only because they were strangers but because, as in her case, she was also a woman. Men like Roy didn't tell women anything, especially a woman he was sleeping with. So, it didn't add up, these true confessions. Caroline could feel something shadowy moving behind it all. She smiled brightly.

'Well, it's very kind of you to offer to get me a ticket on the same flight with you and if you can. Didn't you say you have to go somewhere up north? I've a house in the Lake District. You can come up and stay with me.'

Whatever Caroline felt, she had to stay in there with the plot. Bare boned as it was, it was the only one in town.

Roy hesitated. He liked the idea of being taken to the house – no need of a satnav to get there and then having somewhere to stay. He would slip out in the middle of the night and retrieving the money, drive off. But it was a bit dangerous.

Deciding there and then to take the risk, he nodded agreement, relief breaking through his mask of a face. Caroline was inwardly delighted. He was taking it all – hook, line and sinker. Well satisfied, Roy got up, indicating that he was going to the lavatory. He needed a pee, he said, but he also needed a moment to himself to unpack the day's events, go through them. Things were happening too fast.

As soon as he had disappeared up some curving stairs to the toilets, Caroline hurried out into the quiet street. Moving quickly into an unlit corner of waste ground, she pulled a small mobile phone from her bag. Firing it up with the thumb on her right hand, she tapped out a long tail of numbers.

'Hello Felix. Sorry for waking you, but things are moving down here. Remember I told you about the phone call, well things …. Yes, I mean today. This afternoon! Well, he's going and when I said I'd go with him, he fell for it right away – agreed immediately, even offered to get me a ticket on the same flight. If he gets seats we'll be in London tomorrow night and then back up at the house some time the next afternoon or evening.'

Caroline stopped talking, listening.

'Yes, but I don't think it's anything particularly sinister. He's just not smart enough to come up with something like that, just a congenital liar, and anyway I've told him about you. Said you were my cousin, so he'll think you're there keeping an eye on things.'

In answer to another query, she replied, 'No, he isn't suspicious. Not even interested. If he was, he'd have asked more about you, your name for a start.'

She stopped to listen. 'Okay, I'll see you in London, but don't show up while Roy's about.' Pausing again, nodding every so often, saying, 'Okay' or 'Exactly', she finally said goodbye and folded up the little phone and returned it to her handbag, before going back inside.

Roy, seated alone at the table, was looking slightly disgruntled.

'I thought you'd disappeared. Left with one of the gypsies.' Lamely trying to end on a joke.

'No, I went out to get some air. That's all. The smoke was getting to me a bit.'

They sat for a few more seconds in silence until Roy broke it. 'By the way, what's your invisible relative's name? Your cousin. What's he called?' He'd turned to look at her, but his face was a mask of boredom.

'Felix. It's Felix and he's too big to be invisible, I assure you. You haven't met him because he's found a congenial bar nearer the hotel and he's quite conservative in such things, he likes the known way. Unlike his cousin!' And seeing Roy's puzzled expression, she added, 'Me, silly.'

It was nearly five in the morning and only inertia had kept them in the now empty bar. They called it a night and went back to the Blinking Frog. Tomorrow was going to be, they both agreed, a busy day.

CHAPTER SEVEN

Roy travelled light. Actually, it was so long since he'd been back in England, he was no longer sure what to take or to wear and having a secret horror of being out of fashion, he couldn't imagine any of the stuff he now wore would be 'in' back home. He also had a mother who preserved both a wardrobe of his old clothes and an opinion of Roy not broadly shared. She thought he was a 'good boy'. He planned to stay the first night in England with her, then kit himself out in the least dated of his clothes before proceeding north to keep his appointment with the money.

Caroline woke Roy up early to remind him to go for the airline tickets. He was now uneasily aware, lying there trying to summon the will to get up, that he was the medium through which the two women, Caroline and Emma, were now communicating. He hated women with brains even more than he hated women who thought they didn't need his.

Eventually, he pushed himself unsteadily from the bed, the same miscellaneous mess of yellow sheets Emma had enjoyed. Suddenly, he hated beds that were not proper beds – beds without legs and a base board at each end; beds such as this, low and floor bound, lying squat for everyone to lounge on, wiping their shoes on the sheets. But that was the way things were amongst the shifting, shiftless, expat population along the costas of southern Spain. It was going to be a bad day, he could tell, not that many days were ever that good.

By the time he was ready to move, Caroline had already gone. She must have got up and showered before waking him. Now she was out, no doubt in search of breakfast. In his dreams he had heard the water rattling on the shower curtain. He didn't know why she bothered to come back with him, in the last few days she'd never allowed him sex, just pushed him away saying she was tired.

He remembered what Emma had said, that Caroline was here just to keep an eye on him. Well, he didn't believe that for a minute! It was a typical sour grapes thing an ex girlfriend would say. He pulled on the T-shirt he'd worn yesterday and the jeans he'd been wearing for at least a week and went in search of a coffee. He could not even begin to think until he'd got down at least one, if not two cups of heavily sugared café negro.

On his second cup, he noticed Emma watching him from underneath the brim of another extravagant sun hat. She smiled, but in answer Roy looked away. When he looked back she'd gone. He then remembered he was going to ask her for more money for the trip. The flight was at three o'clock and it was already past eleven. The airport was only thirty-five minutes away and he'd be hand held, so no hold baggage to check in. Roy was fond of saying he only took baggage he could run with. It made him seem more interesting, he thought.

Emma was once again outside the Winking Frog when they both finally emerged, blinking in the bright midday sun. Roy had his overnight bag and Caroline carried what looked like a big makeup bag on a shoulder strap.

Emma watched from her hired car, sitting in the rear seat, leaning well back into the shade. She was perfectly relaxed.

As the pair moved off down the street between the beach and the town looking around for a taxi, she got back into the driving seat, waiting until they were nearly out of sight, then cruised slowly after them, stopping only when she came upon them negotiating with the driver of a yellow cab, the only one on the rank. It was now about one o'clock.

She followed them to the airport and once there, pulled up on the far side of the road fronting the long, low terminal building. She lost sight of them behind two large tourist buses that drew up immediately behind their taxi, but this did not bother her; she was not in the business of keeping too close to them and then being discovered herself. She knew Caroline would be keeping an open mind on Roy's story because Caroline never closed the book on anything until it was dead, embalmed and nailed down. It was getting hotter.

Emma had planned to stay there, keeping the entrances to the airport building under observation until their flight left, but after about twenty minutes one of the local police patrolling the airport came up and asked her to move on. She didn't speak Spanish and he didn't speak English, but his purpose was clear so she decided not to wait any longer. Instead, she made two rather perfunctory circuits of the airport complex before it came to her that she was now just as visible to them as they would be to her.

Emma did a U-turn and drove back into the town to her hotel. In her room she settled down to wait for dark. It was all going along nicely, she thought, as she lay on the bed thinking of how the money would change her life. There were about four million dollars of it.

Drifting between uneasy sleep and consciousness, going over the past weeks in her mind, she gradually became less sanguine, more perturbed. There was nothing she could put her finger on to account for this sudden and subtle unease. Maybe it was simply because she was alone in a dark, anonymous hotel room – for things had, in fact, gone remarkably well over the past few days.

Each step had followed the previous one seamlessly with the certainty of predestination, but she must never let her guard down; she was stealing a lot of money from some dangerous and resourceful people.

Emma was not sure if Caroline was capable of murder, although she was certainly capable of ordering it, but Felix was different, he was capable of both. More than capable, he'd think nothing of it. Felix was formable because he seemed not to weigh events. To him ordering a meal or a murder seemed much the same. Felix could always do, as a matter of course, whatever was necessary.

Emma had dinner sent up to her room and settled back again to wait. In these lower latitudes, darkness came quite quickly, but it was after ten before she stirred herself to begin the last act of her plan. Roy and Caroline would be in London by now, maybe even on the way north by car, if that was how they would travel. She doubted that Caroline would take the train. It was too exposed, too outside her control.

Emma smiled. She'd seen the last of that embarrassing couple, each embarrassing in their own way – Roy because he'd simply been conveniently to hand, like a crass fashion accessory, while Caroline was embarrassing because she knew Emma. Knew her too well, knew her history, what Emma had done and could do. With Caroline on the scene it was impossible to tidy up the past – difficult even to rationalise it. She knew Emma's visceral need for money. But money would make her different, she told herself. A different Emma. Any kind of person she cared to be as long as the past could equally be ascribed anew.

Getting into the bar was no problem. Emma had thoughtfully provided herself with a spare key. She had done this simply by losing the original key Roy had given her soon after moving in. She had then, with much contrition, gone out and bought Roy a new lock, ostentatiously refusing a new key, having already taken the precaution, while in the shop, to get an extra one cut.

"Keep it simple", she'd murmured to herself at the time, but keeping it simple was something that in reality she rarely managed.

Inside the bar, she switched on a small pencil flashlight and keeping the beam on the floor, felt her way carefully up the stairs. The stale living quarters above, with the peculiar odour of dirty laundry and talcum powder, caused her to shudder involuntarily. She was glad this would be her last visit to Roy's squalid chambers and, despite knowing that, by now he'd be in another country, she still took care to be as unobtrusive as possible.

Emma had hidden the safety deposit key between two rows of red bricks in the wall directly behind the bed. To get it she had to pull the mattress away from the wall, moving it back enough to allow her to sit on it, but still be within easy reach of the wall. She sat motionless for a full minute, recovering her breath and to familiarise herself with the natural sounds and shades of the environment.

All she heard were noises from the street, a dull base beat that seemed to run through the ragged conflation of music from a dozen bars, punctuated by occasional isolated snatches of conversation borne up on freak acoustic swirls.

Getting to work, she leaned towards the wall and with the little beam of light highlighting the dull red brickwork, counted the bricks along the floor – six in from the corner of the room, then two up. As she counted, she gave a slight smile. Caroline's sleeping head had lain in perfect peace, inches away from the key to all their missing money.

When she'd finished counting, keeping her finger on the mark, she put the torch on the floor directly below and opening a small bag, brought out a nail file. Then crouching forwards on her knees, her back to the unmade bed, she began to search between the bricks with the file. A few seconds later a small discoloured alloy key tumbled out and landed on the floor in front of her left knee.

As she picked it up, a swoosh of relief transfusing her body, she was pushed violently forwards into the wall and a thin wire cut into her throat, closing off the air. She tried to rear up, but was banged violently back down against the wall again, her head smashing back into the brick, her assailant's elbows closing hard on her ribs.

This was the last thing she was to be aware of in this life. The hands holding the garrotte never slackened and in seconds she lost consciousness and within another minute she was dead.

CHAPTER EIGHT

On the aircraft, Caroline and Roy didn't speak much. This was the first time they'd been away from the bar and the beach town together, and they were at a loss for words – suddenly aware of how little they knew each other. Not that it mattered, each assured themselves privately. They were only together, after all, for motives of personal convenience; although the reasons Emma had ascribed for Caroline's presence by his side still troubled Roy. In his perfect conceit, he saw himself cleverly duping Caroline, but simply hadn't the turn of mind to consider her doing the same to him. It was an ignorance that in other circumstances could have made him invincible. Now, it only made him even more vulnerable.

Caroline was equally uneasy about the turn of events; this sudden trip to England by Roy. She always had bad feelings about anything that did not have a clear rationale, and she was beginning to wonder if they were really on the point of recovering the initiative – or were they still being manipulated by Emma?

Roy's sudden and uncharacteristic helpfulness in getting her a ticket on the same aircraft was beginning to nag at her, now that she had the time to sit and reflect on it. Maybe, she should have seen it sooner for she had, almost from the moment of their first meeting, put him down as someone who was foreign to such sudden little gestures and kindnesses. But there was nothing to be done about it now, she decided, but play it out according to the script. The plan was simply to stay close to Roy. He was still their only contact with Emma, and Emma had their money.

Roy wanted to spend the night in London. He said he wanted to see his mother, who lived in Pinner. Caroline, although brought up in London, was rather proud of the fact that she had never knowingly been to Pinner.

'Do you want me to come with you to Pinner? We can take a taxi direct from the airport,' she said again, banking of him saying no.

'No. The Old Lady wouldn't understand. She'd think I was getting married to you or something. She'd also ask about Rita - where she was, etcetera, etcetera. She actually likes Rita. Doesn't know her too well, obviously.'

'Yes, where is Rita anyway? You never said where she was,' asked Caroline.

'I don't fucking know. I've told you before. I'm going to tell my mother she stayed behind to run the bar. It'll kill two birds. Give me the phone number where you'll be staying and I'll give you a call when I get there. I'll have an English mobile by then. You can call me on that.'

'I will call you, but maybe not to night,' she said. 'I might not be in much tonight. I have to see a few people.'

She paused again. 'I could also be delayed a bit tomorrow morning, but I'll let you know and I won't be too late, don't worry. We'll get to the Lake District by tomorrow night.'

Caroline was suddenly afraid that Roy might decide to continue north on his own. She gave him the number of a flat in London she jointly owned with Felix. It was in Chelsea on one of the pricey streets that ran back from the river, close to the Royal Hospital. She intended to pick Roy up in Pinner in a hired car, but that depended on meeting Felix first. He was following them to London on a later flight.

When she got to her flat, having left Roy at Victoria Station, there was a message from Felix saying he'd call later. It was nearly six in the evening and she did have people to see. When she came back, there was another message from him saying he'd been delayed and would probably go straight up to the Lake District. She bolted the reinforced outer door securely and was soon asleep.

The first thing she noticed about Roy when they met up the next morning was that he was dressed in a fashion that had enjoyed a brief flowering about a decade earlier. She surmised that it was the work of his mother and was again glad they were travelling in the relative privacy of a car. "He's my rough trade," she thought and having thus dealt with her private embarrassment, turned her mind back to the plan.

The plan was simple, to get Roy to the Lake District and wait there until Felix caught up with them. She had not expected Felix to either keep close touch with them or turn up when expected. As a matter of policy, he avoided routine of any kind, 'Makes you vulnerable,' he said. 'You lived longer if they don't expect you.'

Privately, Caroline supposed such utterances were feed for his romantic side, but she never took him up on it. It was better not to with Felix, for as well as a romantic side, he also had a ruthless side. Lacking contact with Felix simply led her to assume that nothing had happened that required updating or changing the plan – which was to deliver Roy safely to the house in the Lake District and then wait developments.

They arrived late in the evening, Caroline exhausted after discovering that Roy, an apparently confident driver, suffered sudden, terrifying lapses in concentration. She had early on, and not too politely, taken over and driven the rest of the way. The house was quiet when they arrived. She let them in and after sitting in a large kitchen over a cup of tea, showed him to an empty bedroom, one that happened to have bars across the window. Then glad to be back in her own room at last, she went to bed and was soon asleep.

The next morning over breakfast, Caroline having knocked on his door about nine o'clock to make sure he did not miss it, Roy was introduced to the other occupants of the house. Felix, to whom every one deferred to in varying degrees, had arrived sometime in the night. Roy also met a man called Harry, who Caroline, with a wry smile, introduced as her cousin.

'Another one?' Roy asked. 'Or were you the one I didn't meet in Spain?'

Caroline smiling demurely and glancing round at the other two, who after brief nods, had remained silent, said: 'We're all cousins here, but Felix was the cousin you nearly met in Spain. Sorry about that, but he found other things to do further down the strip so never made it to the Winking Frog. But, in any case,' she finished, 'we're a large and close family here.'

This was greeted by wintry smiles from the other two. Roy decided to shut up.

'So,' said Felix, once Roy had provided himself with a full English breakfast, including two fried eggs, 'are you over for business or pleasure?' glancing fleetingly at Caroline.

'A bit of business, actually. I'm over here to pick up something for a friend and take it back to Spain. Glad to get away from the bar for a while.'

'But it's the middle of the tourist season, isn't?' asked Felix.

'Not quite. But I'm out to earn a few bob from this little errand and I'm only going to be away a few days.'

'Well, anyway, welcome to Burnfoot – that's the name of this house. You'll find there isn't much going on here. We live a very quiet life. Nothing much ever happens. Isn't that right, Caroline?' Felix said, smiling across the table at her.

Caroline returned the smile, but it was more of a reflex, a grimace. Roy felt that these leaden conversational passes were so familiar to them they could have been scripted. He put it down to Felix's trying to impress with his cleverness. Roy always made a point of being unimpressed by people he suspected might be brighter or better educated. "They're all wankers," he'd remind himself to restore his equilibrium.

Harry never opened his mouth throughout the meal, except to eat.

After breakfast, Caroline took Roy down to the village. It was about two miles away and as they wandered through the leafy lanes, the subject came round to the residents of Burnfoot.

Roy asked: 'Where does everyone fit in? It seems an odd party. There's your cousin Harry, who doesn't say much, and then there's Felix, who thinks he's pretty smart and then there's you, the mystery women who turns up on holiday in Spain. What brings you all to this house in the Lake District? Are you on to some scam or…,' he paused for a second, 'Maybe planning one?'

Roy stopped and looked at her. He was relaxed for the first time since leaving Spain.

'We are neither on a scam or planning one,' Caroline said virtuously. 'Nothing that exotic. Felix is a knockerboy from Brighton and Harry's his man – assistant and driver. Felix lost his licence a few years ago for drunk driving and…' she paused to give the statement weight, 'being an antique dealer, he needs to get around and so Harry drives him. You do know what a 'knocker boy' is, don't you?'

She looked at him quizzically before continuing: 'knocker boys relieve the old and the stupid of their family heirlooms. They base themselves in an area for a few weeks and go round knocking on likely houses, detached but run down establishments, looking for forgotten or unrecognised antiques or paintings, things like that. Although not very edifying, there's nothing sinister about it.

"I came up here because I'm in the same business. The antique business, that is, but I have to say I've never been "on the knock" myself, as it's called. That's why we're all here, to make money from antiques.'

'So, you went to Spain from here and you left in the middle of your business – just left it to go on holiday. Was it a bit of a sudden decision?' Roy was looking at her, a mocking twist to his face.

'The antique business, unlike the pub trade, is not seasonal. I went to Spain because Felix came down with the flu and we couldn't carry on without him. It's a very specialised business. Not everyone can walk into a strange house and in half an hour persuade the occupants to part with generations of family treasure.'

'You mean con them out of the family heirlooms,' Roy interrupted. 'I know what a knockerboy is. I just didn't think it was still legal. I thought they'd brought laws in to stop professional dealers taking advantage of all those senile old pensioners holed up in all these old country houses.'

Caroline looked at him for a moment. He was right of course. They had brought in laws and that was one reason why they were no longer in the antique game. It wasn't worth the risk; hadn't been for years now.

'Yes, there are laws and we don't break them. We give them a fair price and if we make more than we estimated for them, we get in touch and make it up.'

'I'll bet you do. Every time! Who do you think you're talking to? If you're still on the knock then I don't see any of the tat lying around – and amongst it are bound to be some big pieces as well. And I don't think you were in Spain for your health either. There are a few things I'm still not getting…' he paused, before continuing, 'but I'm slowly getting there, all the same.'

Roy was still smiling. Coming back to England seemed to have done wonders for both his brains and his confidence.

CHAPTER NINE

Caroline was asleep and she was having a bad dream. She was shopping in Harrods and from every department she could see that the stock in the next was even more sumptuous and compelling. She would hurry on in, only to be inexorably drawn on to the next. Although having the compulsions and rhythms of a nightmare, it should have been the antitheses of one, as Caroline was a shopaholic. But it had morphed into one and she was not unhappy to be woken.

Felix was shaking her. The bedside light was already on and when she came to, he had his finger pressed across his lips.

'There's someone in the lab,' he whispered and motioned for her to dress.

Feeling a weight against one leg, pressing down through the blankets, she glanced down. There was a nine-millimetre pistol lying on the cover. It had a silencer already screwed into place. Felix had a torch in one hand.

Caroline climbed out of bed and started to dress.

'What time is it?' she asked, turning to look at her bedside clock. It was nearly four o'clock. 'Who do you think it is? Is Harry awake?'

'I didn't call him. It's probably a false alarm. A micro switch has gone live or something. Maybe even a fox.'

'A fox!' Caroline stared at him incredulously. 'It's more likely to be the police or the fucking customs officers than a stray bit of wild life.'

'It's not the police, I don't think. None of the outside alarms went off. It's only the one at the entrance to the shed. Come on, we'll soon find out.'

'And what about Roy? Did he hear anything? If he didn't we'd better keep him out of it.' She was pulling on a pair of dark trainers over her pyjamas.

Felix stared at her, exaggerating his amazement at this suggestion.

'He doesn't even come into it. It's fuck all to do with him. He knows nothing and we'll keep it that way.'

There was a degree of menace in his tone. Picking up the hand gun from the bed, he turned away without another word. Caroline went to a cupboard and, arming herself with a smaller weapon, followed him out of the room. They silently made their way out through the back door of the main house and down the garden towards the apparently abandoned summerhouse with the yellow door. The night was dark except for the uncertain light from a fitful moon.

As they came up to the summerhouse, a dull light suddenly illuminated it from within, a flickering glow that lasted hardly a second. Felix stopped in his tracks, putting his hand back to stop Caroline walking into him. They paused, stock still for a few seconds.

Carefully putting the torch under his arm and with the other free hand, Felix reached out and very slowly turned the knob to release the catch. He let it hang there, slightly ajar and then, moving back a half step, kicked it open while simultaneously switching on his torch. In the beam, crouched on the floor and looking over his shoulder like a fox fixed in a gin trap, Roy's expression was raw with shock and surprise.

Felix laughed as he leaned over to turn the light on in the shed. But there wasn't much humour in the laugh.

Roy slowly got to his feet, licking dry lips, eyes flickering back and forth between them. He had already noticed the heavy pistol in Felix's hand. Caroline, coming in behind Felix, stood slightly off to one side. She had tucked her weapon in the waistband of her pyjamas. For a few moments no one spoke, then Roy said. 'It's not what it seems.'

Felix smiled and, glancing at Caroline, said: 'It's not what it seems, Caroline. Did you hear that? It's not what it seems. Which is funny as it looks exactly what it seems!' He paused, never taking his eyes off Roy.

'Suspicious! Very suspicious!' he went on. 'Our valued house guest, who is over from Spain on some private business, is found by his hosts trying to pull up the floor of their summerhouse at four in the morning. And he says, "It's not what it seems." Bit of an understatement... if it means anything at all. Unless, of course, you're auditioning to be our new gardener. Are you?'

Felix stopped and silence took over in the dark little space. Finally, he added, 'I think we'd all better go back to the house and talk about this – don't you think?'

Felix was still smiling. He seemed to have all the time in the world. Caroline nodded. She was also now smiling brightly. Felix stood to one side and with a little motion of the hand gun, indicated for Roy to lead the way.

The walk back along the dark path to the main house was silent and slow, Felix and Caroline hanging back, preserving a safe distance between themselves and their guest. Once in the big front room, Felix indicated one of the deep armchairs to Roy, again using the gun. He and Caroline remained standing until Roy was safely seated before crossing over to a stack of hi-fi equipment. After a moment's thought he switched on the radio, turning the volume down. Then crossing back, he stood directly across from Roy.

'So, what were you digging for?'

As he spoke he looked thoughtfully at the gun in his hand, as if noticing it for the first time, before adding, still in the same conversational tone, 'It must have been on Emma's instruction. You were looking for the money she told you was there. That's why you're here – to get our money. The money she stole from us.' As Felix stopped speaking he looked directly at Roy. 'Was that it?'

Roy said nothing. He was sitting bolt upright as if trying to touch as little of the chair as possible. His lips were dry and he licked them constantly. Then he began, almost in a whisper, 'I don't know what you're talking about. I came here for Emma. She said she used to work with you and that she'd left her money somewhere here. In the area. Then she called tonight and said that the map for finding it was in a box in the summerhouse. I didn't know anything about it being your money. I didn't even know it was money.'

As he spoke Roy was trying desperately to remember how much he'd told Caroline; if he had said it was money. Now he found that he couldn't think straight with Felix sitting opposite him and casually gesturing with a large and deadly looking handgun.

Felix glanced at Caroline and laughed.

'That won't wash, I'm afraid, Roy. You didn't get a call tonight...' he held up his hand to silence Roy who was starting to protest, 'because we have the SIM card from your mobile phone so no calls could have come through for you. We swapped it over after you arrived and then switched it off. No, you came here to dig up our summerhouse.'

He paused again for a long second. 'And dig it up you will. Shall we go back to the summer house?' Felix pointed out towards the garden. 'Switch off the alarms, Caroline. We don't want to wake Harry up.'

Gesturing for Roy to get up out of his chair, they all trooped back out to the summerhouse, the sight of which, in the narrow beam of Felix's flashlight, had become even more sinister for Roy.

'Pull up the floor again, please and let us see what Emma wanted you to find.'

They stood behind him while Roy stooped down and caught the hessian bag which, in the light of the shed's single bulb, confirmed the accuracy of Emma's sketch. He pulled it back carefully to reveal ordinary wooden flooring.

'Use this,' said Felix, handing him a short tire lever, 'along that seam,' pointing to an almost invisible edge running across the floor. 'Prise it up and lay it back against the wall.'

Roy took the tyre lever from Felix, weighing it in his hand for half a second, wondering if he could use it to knock him out and escape - but Felix, anticipating him, moved back half a step out of effective range. Roy obediently prised the panel up and below it lay the clear outline of a trap door, held shut by an intricate implanted lock.

Felix leaned forward and handed him a key. 'Unlock it and give me the key back,' he ordered, gesturing with the hand gun.

As it opened, a light came on automatically and Roy found himself looking down into a sizeable wood-lined room, its walls unbroken by any aperture or door. In the middle was a desk and an office chair while off to one side were a bunk bed and a fridge.

'What you see is what you get – my secret room where I come to write my masterpieces. Like Somerset Maugham, I don't like being distracted by a view. Unfortunately, unlike him, mine is not of Cap Ferrat,' he said to a bemused Roy. 'There's even a bed down there and a small fridge.

'There's plenty to eat and drink. In fact, it's quite comfortable, more so than that little slum in the sun you call home – or so I'm told. There's also no way out after we've locked the trap door, so don't go banging or making a noise or smashing anything up or I'll have to come down and kill you.'

Felix paused. 'You can either look on it as temporary digs or your mausoleum, just as you wish. You'll be very comfortable while you wait for Emma to join you.'

Felix finished, giving Roy the gentlest nudge in the back with the revolver. There was nothing more said as Roy slowly climbed down. He stopped at the bottom and looked up just as Felix dropped the trapdoor back into place. As the trapdoor clicked shut, the light went out.

CHAPTER TEN

Back in the house, Felix woke Harry and briefly filling him in on the events of the last two hours and told him to keep an eye on the entrance to the laboratory, adding that he needed time to decide what to do with Roy.

Harry, fresh from a deep sleep, sat blinking through Felix's discourse, looking round as if surprised by his surroundings.

Felix studied him in silence for a few moments before leaving, wordlessly, to join Caroline in the main house. He poured himself a drink, saying, 'Well, what do you make of it all?'

Caroline was nursing a mug of tea in both hands. Without looking up, she said, 'I feel a bit of a fool actually. That call I took from Emma, the one meant for Roy, it's quite plain now that this was an elaborate hoax, a distraction to get me out of Spain!'

She paused, still deep in thought. 'So typical of Emma! She got that poor sap to come here with tales of untold riches. But why she also had him break into the lab as well, I can't fathom – unless it was another of her typically sadistic little twists.' Caroline looked up as she finished.

Felix regarded her in silence for a few seconds. 'Maybe she wanted you both out of Spain. Which would suggest to me that the money must still be there, in that bar.' He looked at her searchingly. 'But it's now too late, she's probably off with it and sunning herself on a beach in the Caribbean. Four fucking million dollars! She was always a smart bitch.'

Caroline straightened up, looking across at Felix with new attention.

'No, that's what she'll want us to think. We must go back down to Spain right away. A S A P!' She spelt it out. 'Things with her are never that simple! She was always one to gild the lily, couldn't help it, but this is far too elaborate even for her – getting both Roy and me out of the country together.

'If the money was that accessible, she'd have gone in and got it while we were both at lunch or something. I've no doubt she has keys for the bar. No, she needed more time to do whatever she had to do to get the money back, otherwise even she wouldn't have gone to such lengths as this. That would be insane. I think we should go back down there and we should go today.'

Felix shrugged and looked away. He began to speak before changing his mind and lapsing back into silence once again, plainly considering what Caroline had just said.

'I think we would be wasting our time. She's had three days start on us already. You can go if you like, but I'll stay here and sort out the problems of the dimwit in the lab. I think we may have to permanently dispose of him. He already knows too much.'

He reached across and took a cigarette out from a carton lying on the table and lit it, inhaling the first draught leisurely. 'Thank God the lab itself is concealed and he can't get into it; doesn't even know about it. But we can't leave him locked down there forever with Harry watching him – if we actually can trust Harry to get anything right. In fact, I think we'll have to do something about Harry. He's becoming a bloody liability.'

'You handle it,' Caroline nodded. 'I don't want to know, so don't give me the details.'

That settled it, Caroline was to go back to Spain and see what she could salvage while Felix dealt with Roy.

'You'd better get some sleep,' said Felix. 'I'll go and check on Harry, make sure he's on the ball keeping an eye on the lab and not letting our guest escape.'

Downing his drink in one hasty gulp, he made his way to the back door. Harry was slumped on a chair, fast asleep, his head turned to one side and his face flat on the kitchen table. Annoyed, Felix shook him but he only groaned. He surveyed Harry silently for a few moments before giving up any attempt to revive him. Then leaving by the back door, he made his way to the shed in the garden.

Pulling up the fake floor, he satisfied himself that the trap door was locked down before returning to the kitchen. Harry was where he'd left him, now back fast asleep across the kitchen table.

Felix stood looking down at him, disdain writ clearly across his face. Harry was now taking so many drugs; he had become a liability. Tired, and seeing that there was nothing more he could do, Felix went back up to bed and almost immediately slipped into a deep sleep.

The next he knew, he was awakened by the sound of footsteps hurrying along the garden's gravel path. He swung out of bed and crossed to the window. Daylight was creeping across the landscape, but there was nothing to see. He stood hesitating before pulling on some clothes to go down to investigate.

Passing the kitchen, he noted with some relief that Harry had gone. "Hope he has finally woken from his stupor!" He thought.

Out in the garden he looked around, his eyes quickly adjusting to the dim light of approaching dawn. Satisfied all was normal, he made his way silently back to the shed, treading very lightly on the shifting gravel. Ahead of him he saw that the top light was back on and instantly slipped his hand into his jacket pocket and reached for his gun.

Inside the shed, the trap door was open. Approaching carefully, Felix leaned over and looked down the hatch. At the bottom of the ladder, Harry was pulling himself slowly to his feet, obviously in a daze.

'What's going on? What's happened?' Felix snapped.

Harry slowly looked up, focusing his eyes. 'I don't know, I came down here to check on him and he came out of nowhere and hit me over the head with something. I think he's gone,' he said, looking around confused.

As Harry was speaking, Felix noticed a small, transparent packet of white powder lying near his feet.

'I'll tell you what you've been doing,' Felix, suddenly furious, shouted down the hatch. 'You didn't come here to check on Roy. You came down here to get some coke. It's lying at your fucking feet.'

Harry, hanging onto the ladder to steady himself, looked up and opened his mouth to speak. A loud bang suddenly resounded, echoing around the small chamber, as Felix shot him between the eyes. Blood and brains spurted out onto the wooden desk behind and he fell slowly backwards.

CHAPTER ELEVEN

Caroline came awake with Felix bending over her. She saw it was daylight.

'Okay, okay, I'm awake,' she said as she pulled herself up from the pillow. 'What time is it anyway? It will take me ten minutes to get ready...' Then noticing Felix's face, she stopped speaking. It was carved in stone.

'What's the matter? Has something happened? What's going on?'

'Harry's dead! Shot in the head.' Felix paused for a long moment, 'And Roy's gone. Don't know how he did it, but I think we should get away from here now!'

As he spoke, Felix was looking out of the window as if expecting to see the forces of law and order swarming towards them across the fields.

'That fucking Roy must have an accomplice. The little rat,' Felix went on, and seeing the confusion on Caroline's face added, 'It could have even been Emma, I don't know any more, but you'd better get up. I'm going back out to move Harry out of sight. We have to lock up and clear out now, get away from here for a while.'

As he reached the door, Caroline stopped him, saying, 'Maybe you're right, maybe it was Emma. Maybe she's been here all the time. If she has it means that the money is here as well – was here, anyway.'

She paused, her mind racing. 'Perhaps it was in the lab after all. Maybe she came back for it after all.'

Caroline swung her feet onto the floor and sat pushing her hair back, her face a study in consternation. Then a look of horror engulfed it.

'My God! That's why they killed Harry. The money was down there and we only went and locked him up with it. They got the money and are half way back to Spain with it now.'

From the door, Felix had turned to examine her, silent for a few seconds while he considered how to respond.

'Well, we can always have a look. Look for where it was – for any new digging. It will be obvious. Let's go and see if you're right.'

Harry was temporarily forgotten as Caroline followed Felix out to the lab, until looking down the hatch, she saw his blood soaked body spread eagled at the bottom of the ladder. Shuddering with revulsion, she steeled herself to climb down past the body. By the time she'd reached the bottom of the ladder, carefully averting her eyes, Felix was already pulling open a steel door concealed behind a panel at the far end of the chamber.

Hooking back the door, they passed through into the narrow drugs laboratory beyond and began hurriedly looking for newly turned earth, for any signs of recently excavations. There were none.

'Curiouser and curiouser,' Caroline kept saying until Felix told her to shut up. There was nothing new to see down there, they agreed. Locking the secret steel door behind them and edging past Harry again, they climbed back up to the garden shed and returned to the house. Once in the kitchen and the door carefully closed, Caroline asked: 'Was the door to the lab locked?'

Felix shook his head. 'No, it was unlocked, but that doesn't mean they unlocked it. It could have been Harry looking for dope that let them in – and come to think of it, there's plenty places Emma could have hid the money in the lab without digging a hole. We just never thought of it. Too fucking obvious!'

'So, what do we do now?' Caroline asked. 'If they have the money and they killed Harry, they certainly won't stick around.'

'I think I should go back to Spain as soon as possible to watch Roy, see if Emma's about or if he's getting ready to run...' Felix broke in, but Caroline interrupted him,

'No, I think we should both go, there's nothing for us to do here and with all that's happened I'll feel safer away from here – and he's the only lead we have. I can always keep in touch with the daily on goings from there, get her to come over a couple of times a week to do a bit of cleaning and keep up a semblance of normality.'

Looking fixedly at Caroline, Felix butted in: 'But I don't think you should go back to Spain. You're too well known down there now. If Roy or any of his friends spot you, they might call the police. I think we should close up here and you should go off somewhere quiet until it's all over. Okay, Roy knows me now, but no one else down there does. I'll go down and see if he's still there, but keep out of sight. There's nothing much else we can do here.'

'They're not going to call the police anyway – after killing Harry,' Caroline came back in. 'I can't get a clear take on it anymore; there's too many possibilities now, and anyway, it won't be in Emma's interests to have Roy on the loose, not now. The best she can do is to pay him off and move on, unless of course, there is a third person involved, someone else has materialised out of the blue, so to speak.'

Caroline paused for a moment. 'But I doubt it and it doesn't matter anyway. Once Emma pays Roy off, he's out of it. He's not a player anymore, so we must get down there before this happens.'

Felix could not persuade Caroline to stay behind. She didn't want to be at the Lake District house on her own, she said, and she didn't want to get too far from the money either so, when it came down to it, she kept repeating, their best course of action, with all these unknowns, was for them both to go to Spain as soon as possible to see if Roy was there – and to look for Emma. And so it was settled, they would both go to Spain in the morning.

Felix left her to go back and sort out the body. Caroline watched him walk up the pathway towards the shed. She turned and closed the door. She didn't want to know the details.

From Madrid, they caught a local flight to the coast and taking a taxi from the airport, chose a hotel recently thrown up in an area used mostly by German tourists. After a brief supper, they went to bed. Felix, not in the best of moods, assuring himself that tomorrow was another day.

CHAPTER TWELVE

Further down the beach, Roy and his wife Rita were sitting in the tiny sitting room above the bar. At first, too afraid to return after his escape from the dungeon in the Lake District, he'd spent the night in a grimy hostel further down the beach and with his money running out, decided to loop past the bar to see what was going on.

To his surprise it was open and quite busy. Entering, he discovered Rita behind the bar exchanging banter with a few determined customers. The reunion was brief and remarking to his wife, 'So the boyfriend threw you out?' Roy parked his bag back up in the bedroom.

That afternoon in the brief period when the Winking Frog closed before the evening's business began, he offered her an edited account of his absence – considering it need not be too detailed in view of her own time away.

Roy told Rita he'd been recruited by a mystery woman he'd met in the bar to go to the Lake District and recover her money with the promise of a large reward, but nothing had come of it and it appeared more a fantasy than anything. But at least he wasn't completely out of pocket, she'd given him five hundred euros.

He omitted any mention of the garden shed or his own temporary incarceration there, just saying that when he got to the house, it had changed hands and he was unable to make contact with the person he was supposed to meet.

There were other reasons for his reticence – Roy still hadn't come completely to terms with his escape. He was still bemused by it. Sitting forlornly at the bottom of the narrow entrance shaft, at a loss to do anything but stare into the haunted darkness, he'd been taken completely by surprise when the light came on and instinctively moved off into a dark corner.

Seconds later the trapdoor had been thrown open and one of the men he'd met in the house began to descend the ladder. He recognised him as the silent 'cousin'. Roy remained frozen with fear in the dark corner until he realised that the other man had obviously not seen him because as soon as he reached the bottom of the ladder, he'd crossed to one of the walls and began running his hands up and down it as if he was looking for a secret compartment. Sure enough, a small door sprung open and the man removed a small package and began turning it over carefully in his hand.

Roy waited no longer. Picking up a small crowbar he noticed leaning against the wall, he came quickly up behind the man and hit him over the head, knocking him out cold. With hardly a moment's hesitation, he was up the ladder and legging it along the garden path, the gravel crunching under his frantic footsteps. Coming on a low garden wall, he threw himself across it and was gone.

In the welcoming darkness, he had begun to sense the outline of some master plan, too much was going on, his escape was too easy, as if choreographed. He was the merest pawn in something he couldn't even begin to understand.

The main house remained reassuringly in darkness as Roy made his rapid flight across the fields and into a dark wood. Hours later, on a county road, he stopped a bus and asked its bemused driver where the nearest railway station was – and so began his empty return to Spain, via his now distraught mother in London.

Rita in turn, had explained her absence by saying she'd gone back to her mother to get away from the bar, the beach town and Roy for a while. This was probably true, Roy thought. Now, she said, she was back to get them both through the summer and then they would sell the bar as a going concern, split any profit and go their separate ways.

'Suits me, I'm outward bound myself,' Roy replied and so it was left at that, an uneasy silence now pervading the little sitting room, a room so cramped that they used to joke that at least they didn't need a remote control for a television.

But the time for such jokes or indeed any jokes, had passed for both of them. Now communicating mostly with grunts and glares, they were bound together by poverty and the raw memories of recent deceits, having both come home empty handed, back to the life of grind and misery and now both hating themselves, each other and their customers in equal measure.

These feelings were too graphic to conceal from their customers, but oddly enough, in such a sensory desert, a quarrelling couple behind the bar became an attraction, giving the regulars the opportunity to both scold and mock while feeling better about themselves.

Soon the word went round and the Winking Frog began to prosper – for even the most transitory of tourist bars needs regulars, if only an endlessly shifting core lasting only the duration of an annual holiday. For the first time in its short history, the Winking Frog was threatening to become a success.

At nights, if they stayed in after closing, usually through a shortage of cash, they'd sit in the kitchen conversing in monosyllables, their discussions invariably edging towards the causes of their common plight. The conclusion, with small variations, was always the same – that Roy had been completely fooled by Emma right from the get go.

Rita would point out how Emma had been happy at first that Roy was there in the bar, running it from day-to-day. Then quite suddenly she'd wanted him out of the bar, out of the town, out of Spain even, and had gone to lengths that defied comprehension to achieve this, because, 'What had been the point of sending him first to England and then to the Lake District?' Rita would ask, when whatever purposes Emma had in their bar could surely have been achieved in an hour or two.

There was no evidence of any significant changes or alterations to the bar or the rooms upstairs, suggesting that she hadn't needed much time to do whatever it was she had to do.

Then it came to Rita. 'Of course, it wasn't you she needed out of the way, it was that woman Caroline, wasn't it? She needed her away from here and the only way she could be sure of doing that was by getting you back to England as well, sudden like. She knew that Caroline would have to follow you.'

Rita stopped to think. 'Of course sending you to the very house where they'd all lived was her master stroke. Right away they'd think that the money was still there!' She paused, shaking her head out of respect for Emma. 'She wasn't stupid, that one. It's all falling into place now.'

'Of course she knew Caroline would go with me,' retorted Roy. 'That's what all the fucking stuff with making a show of getting the tickets was about, so that she'd take me back to the house in the Lake District.'

Roy stopped, his thoughts in overdrive as new and uncomfortable ideas began to push their way forwards.

'No, she didn't need Caroline to take you anywhere in particular.' Rita broke in. 'Going to the house in the Lake District was just icing on the cake for Emma. At the end of the day, she only wanted you both out of here, maybe you in particular out of Spain. She could've told you anywhere in England. She came up with the house in the Lake District to give herself a laugh, I suppose!'

Rita finished with a triumphant little smirk in his direction. Its meaning was all too clear – he was the mug's mug once more!

Roy found himself, to his fury, blushing red from ear to ear. He felt like hitting her in the middle of her face, but natural discretion stopped him because, for the moment, they had to sleep in the same bed and work in the same bar and it wasn't as if he didn't have to turn his back on her a hundred times a day.

Later that night as she lay in bed beside her sleeping husband, her mind ranged back over the events of the last few weeks. She could dimly perceive some single prime motive behind it all.

The more she went over it the more it seemed that Roy had been included almost on a whim, but she couldn't discern a good reason for it. It was almost as if he'd been included simply because he was there.

Eventually, still turning such thoughts over in a fruitless treadmill, she fell asleep.

CHAPTER THIRTEEN

Back at the other end of the beach and well away from the Winking Frog, Felix had a problem. He still wasn't any closer to getting hold of the money and as he spoke no Spanish, he had an overwhelming sense of impotence. He felt that in such a volatile situation, he needed to be up with every nuance of the language.

Caroline spoke passable Spanish and even looked a bit like Emma, but she wouldn't do for what lay ahead. Felix had no intention of letting her into the twist that included the demise of Emma because it would mean sharing the money with her. He didn't intend to share it with anyone.

He decided that as he was not under pressure, he'd play a longish game, sit there in the hotel with Caroline and pretend to believe that sooner or later they would either run into Emma or discover something of her whereabouts. He intended to wait patiently until Caroline, gradually became aware of the pointlessness of the plan, got fed up and went back to England.

This took over a week before Caroline, who was keeping in touch with their 'daily' cleaner back in the Lake District for any news of the untoward, declared that waiting in this dreadful little beach town was a lost cause. She said they should return to England and get on with their lives.

Felix gently objected, coming over as uncertain and undecided, saying that he thought that one of them should wait for a few more days at least – but yes, maybe it would be better if one of them went back to the house to keep an eye on things there.

Caroline went online and booked a flight to the UK and the next morning they shared a taxi to the airport, Caroline thinking it a nice gesture, Felix wanting to be sure she'd left, to wave goodbye to her for what he hoped would be the last time.

In the single terminal building, a long flat structure that included both Arrivals and Departures with travel and car hire booths along one side, Caroline made straight for the check-in queue, telling Felix he needn't wait.

'No trouble,' Felix answered. 'I'll have a cup of coffee with you after you've checked your stuff in.' And he left her to shuffle patiently forwards in a long queue to the Manchester check-in desk.

He was on his second cup when Caroline showed up, all checked in, saying, 'I'll be back in a minute, just going to the loo,' and left in the direction of the lavatories.

Felix hadn't replied, only nodding in acknowledgement as he scanned a free local tourist guide taken from a pile by the checkout till. Coming back a few minutes later, he glanced up to acknowledge Caroline and froze. Behind her and walking towards the coffee counter was Emma. The same Emma he had garrotted and left dead not so long ago in the bar.

Caroline stared at him, a question plain on her face. Pulling himself together and straightening his face with some difficulty, Felix mumbled something about a sudden chest pain. Caroline returned to studying the menu card, asking Felix if the coffee was any good.

He could only nod, his mind now going like an electric mixer – it could not be Emma, but who was it?

After more scrutiny of the menu card, Caroline said she'd get herself a 'café solo'. In an instant Felix was on his feet and half-way to the bar, announcing over his shoulder that he'd get it. Caroline, a little surprised at his unwonted good manners, smiled at his retreating back.

At the bar Felix, positioning himself for a closer look at the Emma look-a-like, realised that although the likeness was almost uncanny, she was younger and prettier than the original. It took him a very few seconds to conclude that she might be a younger sister.

He turned his mind back, furiously trying to recall if Emma had ever mentioned a sibling – but all he could remember was her once saying, quite distinctly, that she was an only child. But the likeness was uncanny. Then it came to him – could this woman, obviously here on holiday, be the breakthrough he needed, the key to recovering the money. She could be Emma's sister – as far as the bank was concerned!

Almost as instantly, he knew he mustn't let her out of his sight. Beside a sizeable dark cloth hand bag, there was a suitcase on the floor by her side.

The barman placed Caroline's coffee in front of Felix and he automatically paid for it. Back at the table, he announced that maybe he wouldn't wait to see Caroline off, but would make his way back to town.

'You'll be okay?' He asked in mock solicitude.

Caroline laughed in his face. 'Of course I'll be okay. I can get aboard an aeroplane myself you know. I'm a big girl now.'

They kissed, said goodbye and Felix passed out of sight through the entrance to the coffee shop. He didn't go far, but found a position where he could watch the Departure Lounge without being too obvious.

A few minutes later the girl (for she was hardly a woman yet) appeared, wheeling her suitcase. She stopped for a moment in the bright day and looked about her, taking stock of her surroundings, before continuing slowly towards the row of taxis parked along the pavement.

As soon as he saw her talking to a taxi driver, Felix hurried past, keeping against the terminal wall, hoping against hope that he'd get a driver that understood a little English. He realised that the recovery of his money hinged on as little as this.

His luck was in. Explaining that he wanted to keep the other taxi in sight, the driver nodded cheerfully and as the other taxi pulled away from the kerb, the cabbie took up station behind it.

All the way into town Felix remained on tenterhooks, only allowing himself to relax when the taxi in front pulled up at a small hotel in a street some way back from the beach. He watched the girl get out, collect her suitcase from the driver and after paying him, drag it up the short flight of steps into the hotel.

Carefully noting the name of the hotel, Felix leant forwards and instructed the driver to take him to his own hotel. Once there, he tipped him heavily and taking the man's business card, stowed it in his wallet. He could be a useful contact.

Back in his room, he called room service. He was in a state of nervous elation. The game was back on again as he now had his stand-in for Emma. He also had the key to the safe deposit box where their stolen money had to be deposited – why otherwise would Emma have based her whole elaborate and ultimately, fatal plans, around its concealment and recovery.

All that was needed now was to retrieve the money from the bank safe deposit. He knew the name of the bank, it was on the tag attached to the key. The next step was to somehow persuade this new girl to get the money for him.

Felix's forte was deception – stage magic taken away from the footlights, studied manipulation followed closely, if required, by coercion. His range was complete from looking earnestly at someone with his clear blue eyes while lying effortlessly to, if necessary, calmly killing them moments later without emotion.

All he needed now was a good back story and he'd be gone. He could settle anywhere; he had no close friends, no bailiwick too comforting to give up. Felix had long given up on his own family as hopelessly bourgeois, irredeemable limited.

He lived only for the buzz he got from crime.

CHAPTER FOURTEEN

Jane sat on her sister Emma's bed in the hotel room. She'd already flipped through Emma's things but had discovered nothing to say where she might be. Everything seemed in order; all that was missing were her handbag and passport. Jane sat back, considering what to do now. It was odd that her sister had been away from her room for at least a week now, according to the hotel people, and with only a handbag.

Earlier, when the pair were making arrangement for Jane to join her, Emma told her she'd already booked a double room for them. Since then, on not hearing anymore despite making many fruitless calls, Jane had flown out to see what was going on. She would talk again to the concierge in the morning to ask about her sister and check for any messages. Now, however, she decided to get some sleep.

She was tired from the day's rigours, and contenting herself with some fresh fruit she found in a basket, obviously some courtesy presentation from the hotel, turned in for the night.

Jane tried not to worry. Emma had said that she might have to come and go while Jane was there. Emma had always been of a subtle, secretive nature and so her disappearance was not completely unexpected.

The next morning, she showered, dressed and went down to see about breakfast. She'd been in small Spanish hotels before and knew they often had no dining room. This one did, with breakfast laid out on a side board. She helped herself to some yogurt and rolls and ordered a coffee, then picked a table by a window that looked out on the dusty street. It was still early and there were few people about so she turned her attention back to the dining room.

It was almost empty; a couple at one table, another young woman like herself and a single man in his middle thirties who smiled at her brightly, maybe a little too brightly. Automatically returning the smile, but only as a polite response – she as quickly forgot him.

Turning back to her breakfast, she went over the last hours since her arrival. She still had the uncomfortable feeling that her sister was in trouble and yet had nothing tangible to go on. She resolved to go back up to the room and search through Emma's belongings again.

As she got up to leave, she noticed the man who had smiled at her earlier was still there, watching her. Averting her eyes, she left the room. This was no time to start anything. She was here on business, to find her sister.

Reception was still empty and she didn't want to hang about too long, the man in the dining room having made her uneasy. She would ask about Emma later. Once back upstairs in their room, she went through her sister's things again, looking for any unusual items, any clues to her whereabouts. Nothing of interest surfaced other than a piece of paper that looked like a receipt. It had a logo of a cat and dog coiled in unlikely harmony.

Turning out her sister's makeup bag on to a table, she raked through it, finding herself disturbed that Emma had also gone off for so long without it. No woman went anywhere for any length of time without her makeup. She came across another piece of paper folded around a small key, a key for a briefcase. It was also a receipt, but this time it had the name of a bank across the top, the Caja something.

Below in the main body of the note, were some short printed lines that ended in dots. These lines were ended mostly in illegible scribbles, but on one a number stood out. On this line the word, 'Caja' appeared again. Jane knew this meant a box or a bank. She put the key in her purse and studied the little piece of paper from the bank; these two scraps of paper, the coiled cat and dog and this one, were the only things she could not explain. Everything else was as expected.

Jane lay on the bed, her hands behind her head and more than ever, with a growing impatience, felt that something was not right. She had the receipt for a safe deposit box in a bank and could simply walk in and ask for an explanation, but somehow felt that such an approach would be uninformed and gratuitous – and being uninformed and gratuitous, could equally have unwanted consequences.

There was also the other receipt, the one from a dog kennel, that on the surface looked pretty innocent, a receipt for your dog. She'd go there and make inquires. Her sister was very fond of dogs, preferring them to humans, she often said, so her travelling with one was not necessarily a surprise. This could hardly be a major clue of some dangerous plot, could it?

Heaving herself off the bed, she found the paper from the kennel again. It had a phone number below the name 'K9'. She dialled and almost immediately an English voice answered. Midlands accent, a woman. Jane plumped for Leamington Spa.

'I wonder can you help me,' she said. 'I'm looking for my sister and I think she's left a dog with you.' She hesitated for a moment. 'My sister's name is Emma.'

The voice at the other end, after a suitable pause, answered, 'Clarence. I think we're talking about Clarence. I was wondering why I hadn't heard from her. She used to call nearly every day, asking after Clarence and then one day, must have been a week or so ago, she stopped. I got worried because I didn't think she was like a lot of pet owners, who only have them because they think they should, new life in Spain and all that, then find they have to be fed and walked every day. No, I was worried.'

'She stopped calling over a week ago?' Jane cut in, impatient with the circumlocutions of animal lovers. 'Did she say anything that might give an idea of what she was doing?'

There was a longish silence on the other end and then the lady from K9 kennels continued, with a degree more enthusiasm.

'Well, she did say she was almost ready to leave. She said she had a couple of things to do before she could come for Clarence, but it wouldn't be long.'

'Like a day or two?'

'Yes, about a day or so. Something like that. In fact, she did ask me if she would need any special papers to get him in to Costa somewhere. I think she meant one of these countries in Central America or South America – somewhere like that.'

Jane waited, but the woman couldn't remember anything else, only offering up that it could have been Costa Rica - so after an exchange of the usual pleasantries with Jane promising to collect Clarence soon and settle the account, she rang off.

Now she knew something definitely untoward had happened to her sister. A slow panic spread through her, shutting down her horizons, suddenly making her world smaller and greyer, as if the walls were closing in.

Deciding she could no longer sit in her sister's room letting these dark shadows crowd her mind, she found her handbag and, briefly checking her makeup, left the hotel and began strolling aimlessly towards the beach.

There wasn't much of interest and later, sitting in a nearby café looking out to sea, she decided the first thing she must clear up was if there really was a safe deposit box. There had been no safe deposit key, only a receipt for one and a small key, as for a briefcase. Jane supposed there could be some procedure at the bank where the box was deposited, but not speaking a word of Spanish, she'd need a translator; someone to explain what was going on.

Earlier, ordering a cold drink, she'd noticed a pile of local English language newspapers on the café's counter. Going over, she took one and sitting back down, began methodically leafing through it. It was called the '*The New Euro*' and seemed full of cosy advice on pets, cooking and real estate law interspersed with half-page adverts for property sharks scaring a quaking readership with terrible tales of court sanctioned expropriation, legal demolition and official robbery. Their message was always the same; they must liquidate and rush all their capital to the safety of the advertiser's private offshore fund.

Jane turned to a page of classified adverts, ploughing past columns of desirable property, past people who fitted satellite dishes, past ads for the same men who also fitted burglar alarms and air conditioning, until she came upon a lone entry advertising translation and interpretation services. It said to call Tracy and gave a number. Jane made a note in her Filofax and finishing her drink, went in search of a phone.

There seemed to be no public phones and passing a mobile phone shop, decided to go in and buy one. A few minutes later she emerged, studying a small broad handset with a lid that flipped open.

Then began an awkward bit of juggling, trying to get her Filofax open at the page with Tracy's number, while not dropping the new phone. Finally, giving up and laying it down for a moment on the sloping green top of a public rubbish bin, she found the page and dialled. The call was quickly answered in a breathless little girl's tones, a North American accent.

Jane asked directly. 'Have I got Tracy?'

'Sure, that's me!' Followed by a trilling little laugh that made Jane want to flip the lid of her mobile shut again. But she needed an interpreter and this one, even with a skirling little girl's laugh, was the only one available.

'I need someone who speaks good Spanish to come to a bank with me, to translate for me. Can you do that? Are you available?' Jane waited for an answer.

'Of course! Just tell me when and where and I'll be there!'

'How much do you charge?' Jane always believed in meeting awkward questions early.

There was a pause and then Tracy asked, 'When do you want to go and how long do you think it will take?'

'Oh, about an hour, I should think. It's concerning a safe deposit box and I just want to ask a few questions. Tomorrow would be good.'

'Okay, in that case, I would charge thirty euros!' Tracy ended on a high note and closed the deal with another whinny little laugh.

Jane paused for half a second, looking off down the street at tight lipped, sweating families dragging whining children between ice cream vendors. 'Okay, we'll do it. What about mid-day tomorrow outside the Solamar bank? Do you know where it is? It's the one on the beach road, by a big Italian restaurant.'

'Yep, think I know it. I can find it anyway.'

'Okay,' said Jane. 'I'll give you my phone number so we can keep in touch.'

Here, Tracy cut in. 'That's okay, I've captured it already from this call,' And so they rang off.

Jane now had to think of the line to take in the bank. She decided to march in, to behave as if she knew all about it. As if she was Emma.

It was still early and she decided to go out on the town. She wasn't really an 'out on the town' girl, but she couldn't bear another afternoon lying about in her sister's room, thinking about vague unknowns.

It was hot and getting hotter and she dressed accordingly, a bikini covered by a beach robe stylish enough to pass for a summer dress. Jane had

105

no plans and nothing in particular she wanted to do, so decided on a bit of window shopping until lunch.

Twenty minutes later, she was utterly fed up. Almost all the shops were stuffed with identical tourist tat. Arriving at the bottom of a second street, she realised that she'd had enough of shopping – an unusual girl who could pass a shoe shop as easily as other girls could a machine tool emporium.

Looking down a short street, she could see the beach, yellow and heaving with people. 'Must be a café there!' she thought and thankful that she could drop all pretence of shopping, of being busy, she made her way to the sea.

CHAPTER FIFTEEN

There was a profusion of cafés and bars, ordinary walk-in ones on the landward side of the street and on the other side, beach bars that were so tightly spaced they almost leant against each other. Jane settled on a more permanent looking cafe across the road from the beach that was biggish and busy. Making her way to the very back, she settled on the chair furthest away at a table for four.

She felt as if she was in a movie sculking around like a detective! It was rather fun, but tinged with a big pinch of fear – fear of the unknown stretching ahead. She ordered coffee and a glass of cold mineral water to steady her nerves.

Halfway through the coffee she felt a tap on her shoulder. Looking up, she saw a man beaming down as if he knew her. For a long moment she couldn't place him. Then it came back to her, he was the man in the coffee shop of the hotel that morning who'd exposed her to his thousand watt smile, obviously trying to pick her up.

He said, 'Can I sit down? I thought I recognised you. I saw you at breakfast in the hotel. Hope you weren't put off by my approach.'

Jane shook her head politely and indicated a chair. Instead, he chose one nearer to her. She paused until he was settled and then looked at him inquiringly, waiting for him to explain himself. She hoped it wasn't a pick up. Far too early and she didn't really like such a blatant approach and anyway he wasn't her type, too old and too much the charmer.

'I have a small problem you might be able to help me with. I need someone to go into a bank and recover some things in a safe deposit box.'

'Why don't you do it yourself? They probably speak English and they are…'

Felix cut in, stopping her. 'I need a woman to do it and preferable one who looks like my ex,' he said.

'You want me to impersonate your ex girl friend, go into a bank and open a safe deposit box. Sounds criminal to me!' Jane finished on a rising note, her tone a note of incredulity.

'No, I don't want you to impersonate anyone,' he said in a heavily patient voice, emphasising each word. 'I have the key for a safety deposit box. I just want to check the contents, not to remove anything. To see what she's actually left in it. I want to find out if she took anything that wasn't hers.'

Felix trailed off, all the time looking at Jane closely. 'I'll pay you well!'

In Jane's head, wheels were beginning to mesh. Always believing that coincidence have a limited writ, she began to feel more strongly than ever the presence of a malign synchronicity – it was just too coincidental to be coincidental but she decided to go along with it and not interrogate him further at present. Let it all unwind, she thought, while I've a ring side seat.

'Okay. No problem. I'll do it. You simply want me to go into the bank with you and open a safe deposit box and look inside it. And you're going to pay me?' She looked inquiringly at Felix, who was nodding silently.

'I may not be allowed to go right inside with you as I didn't take it out in the first place,' he said. 'That's why I need you to go ahead and check it out. You're a woman and you look very like her – younger and prettier maybe. You could be her sister.'

Felix allowed himself a tight little smile here. 'So, it might work. It's just a way to find out if it's all there before I have to go to all the bother of getting the proper papers.'

'I can't be her sister. I'm an only child – anyway what should I expect?' Jane interrupted, surprised at her unnecessary lie about having no sibling. It had come from nowhere.

'Here's the thing,' said Felix brushing aside her remark. 'I know what's in the box, or rather what should be in the box, but I don't want to tell you as it may predispose you not to see what's actually there when it's opened.'

He looked at her puzzled expression for a second, before going on. 'Do you get what I'm driving at?'

Jane was nodding and smiling. 'I get the idea. You want me to look in the box with a completely open mind so I see everything that's there – rather than what I should expect to see if you'd told me first!'

Enjoying the interview for the first time, she added. 'I cannot, unfortunately, do it immediately as I've arranged to go out of town, but after that is okay – the day after tomorrow?' She finished, smiling brightly at him.

'Okay, but the sooner the better,' was all Felix said.

He got up, shook her hand rather formally and left without looking back, still the epitome of business-like behaviour.

Jane watched him go and when he was out of sight, found her new mobile phone and bringing up Tracy's number, called it. Almost immediately it was answered and after a brief greeting, Jane confirmed their meeting tomorrow, but brought it forwards to ten, the earliest decent time to meet in Spain. She said something had come up, which indeed it had. Tracy closed by remarking that banks in Spain all closed at two.

It was not yet midday and she had nothing to do until the next morning but wait. She spent the rest of the morning wandering aimlessly about, getting the feel of the town, before going back to the hotel for a siesta. The rest of the day stretched before her and she was reduced to planning a trip to visit her sister's dog that afternoon. She would set out about six. Afternoons in that part of Spain did not begin until about then.

Felix, in the meantime, had returned to his hotel not entirely happy with the interview with Jane. He had little doubt that she would pass muster for her sister. He was equally confident that without an interpreter, a deliberate omission on Felix's part, there would be enough stumbling ambiguity in any conversations with the bank to allow him to promote Jane as Emma – and if exposed, not be nailed down on it.

Felix had benefited in the past from the polite leeway built in to such mutually obstructive conversation. His worry was much less specific. Simply, that it had all gone too well, it had been too easy. He had gone into the meeting expecting she would flatly refuse and maybe walk out – or would have to be bribed with a lot of money. That was it! By all appearances an essentially law abiding 'nice' girl, Jane had gone along with it a bit too easily!

Felix too lay on his bed, adopting a similar pose to Jane, stretched out down the middle, hands behind his head. He had a procedure he often tried when considering a new situation. He would lie back, close his eyes and put his mind to the area of the subject, not actually focusing on any particular aspect, as if he was scanning a landscape. He was after the general feel, and the general feel was that things were not all together in sight.

Getting no further with this wide screen view, he turned to specifics. What should he actually do once inside the bank with her? Should he hand her the key or keep it himself. He decided it would be better if she appeared to the bank people to have custody of it. He should also come across as not overbearing, not too much of the warder. But at the same time he must not let her or the key out of his sight.

That was as far as he wanted to go with forward planning, having been struck at an early age by the old military adage that no plan survives initial contact with the enemy. Felix liked this notion because he was both a planner and a southpaw. Where his schemes left off, Felix would be there on his toes, ready to hit on the break, to counter punch.

He finally dozed off; satisfied that he had done all he could in the circumstances.

CHAPTER SIXTEEN

The next morning prompt at ten, Jane was waiting outside the bank when Tracy bustled up, for some reason carrying a clip board like a pavement psychologist. They went in together and Tracy asked for the manager. It was a small bank and there seemed to be a total of three staff, two tellers and, in an open office behind them, a tall thin gentleman in summer business attire.

The teller Tracy had spoken to picked up the phone and it rang in the open office a few feet away. A few seconds later the thin gentleman stood up, beaming at the sight of two young women.

Tracy launched into a long preamble in Spanish with plainly an American intonation. The manager kept nodding as she explained that Jane would like to look into a safe deposit box – here she proffered the receipt, adding sadly that she had mislaid the key.

The manager, his expression now grave, looked anew at Jane, noticing again how pretty she was. She returned a wide, but appealing smile that said, "Yes, I'm beautiful, but also vulnerable!" It was not wasted, going straight to the manager's heart as he looked on gravely, responding occasionally to the long explanation.

Jane was getting impatient. Tracy was obviously one of those irritating translators who took over the task so completely they often forgot the existence of the principle. Jane gave a screen cough and as they both turned back to her, she asked: 'What's he saying?'

'Oh, he says that you must have a key as well as a receipt to get access to a box and that you'll have to get a replacement one. You'll need to go to a notary and swear that you've lost the original key and then pay the cost of a replacement key.'

Jane glanced across at him. He was smiling encouragingly at her. Tracy continued: 'But he also says that as he remembers you from before when you rented the box, he can let you look through it now and check that everything's there.'

Jane opened her mouth to speak, to say that he was mistaken, that it had been her sister who rented it, and just as quickly closed it again and instead, managed an encouraging nod to both of them.

Smiling broadly the manager made a gesture for them to follow and led them out of a door at the back of the room and down some steps into a vault. Behind another heavy door were rows of safe deposit boxes along three walls. He consulted the receipt again, then led them over to one of the boxes and after much sorting through bunches of keys, eventually settled on one and inserting it into the front of the box, pulled it open.

Inside, occupying most of the box was a red leather brief case. He waved his hand towards it, inviting Jane to take it out and open it. Then he retreated to a chair at the far end of the cellar. Jane stared at the brief case, hesitating, uncertain what to do.

Before she could decide, Tracy stepped forward, nudging her aside and with one deft movement, removed the case from the box.

'The key…,' she hissed, thrusting her hand out. Jane stared blankly at her for a second until she remembered the small key she'd found with the receipt for the box. Diving to the bottom of her handbag and after the lengthy mandatory scrabble, came up with it, and still without thinking, handed it to Tracy.

In a second the briefcase was unlocked and pulling it open, Tracy tipped it forwards to reveal a sheaf of papers, a couple of passports, personal stuff. She looked over at Jane, clearly disappointed, but Jane was staring past her into the depth of the box, now revealed by the removal of the briefcase.

The box was deep and the brief case had been resting on a plain cardboard box. Tracy followed her gaze and then literally dropping the brief case, leaned over and tore the top of the box off. It had been stuck into place with lengths of cello tape and it came away, taking bits of cardboard with it.

The box was densely packed with layers of hundred-dollar bills. Tracy stopped, her mouth open, about to say something, transfixed by the sight of so many old dollar bills and so missed the look of complete stupefaction that had captured Jane's face.

Tracy by then appeared to have completely lost her senses, scrabbling through the money, thrusting her hand to the bottom and turning the contents over as if she were mixing a salad. Jane came back to life.

'Stop that,' she snapped. 'It's not your money. Leave it alone. Please take your hands out of the box.'

Tracy stopped, suspended in space and time, then slowly swung her head around to meet Jane's gaze. Her expression was a mix of exhilaration and greed and Jane realized, at that instant, she now had the additional problem of Tracy on her hands.

'I was only checking what's there,' she said, and gave Jane a beaming smile lasting all of a microsecond. She then slowly withdrew her hands, her body language epitomising near terminal reluctance.

Jane forced the cover back on the box, replaced the briefcase and leaning over, pushed the safe deposit box back into its place in the wall again. It was all getting too much for her. She needed to sit down with a cup of coffee and carefully reassess the situation.

She thanked the manager and watched him lock up the safe door before preceding him up the stairs.

Outside in the street she paid Tracy her fee without a further word to her and they went their separate ways – but not before Tracy took time to assure Jane that an important part of her job was retaining confidences encountered during business and if Jane needed any further translation, or indeed any help at all, to call her anytime, emphasising the 'anytime'.

Jane nodded coldly and turning on her heel made her way back to her hotel. She now knew Tracy would not be easy to shake off. It was still a few minutes short of one o'clock. The bank would be open another hour.

Back at the hotel, Jane stopped long enough to change out of her bright red dress into an altogether less conspicuous one, a little modest beige shift with sleeves. Not appropriate for high season hot weather, but just the thing for moving about discreetly. She also put her hair up into a bob. Jane was adopting a new, more elegant persona. She'd noticed that Tracy was short-sighted.

Once she had completed the transformation, she returned to the bank. In the open plan office, the bank manager was back at his desk and she stood politely in line while he dealt with a Spanish couple ahead of her.

It seemed an age before the couple finally finished their business and left and, her heart beating fast, she took her place opposite him and smiled demurely. It was a moment before he recognised her, and then he smiled back, asking her in English what he could do for her. She leaned forwards and launched into a little speech she had carefully worked on while waiting in line.

'I've found the key – or rather I will have it tomorrow. I will bring both the key and the receipt for the box tomorrow!'

The bank manager was nodding in friendly encouragement.

'But I also have a small problem. My boyfriend will be with me and I hate to say this, but I don't really want him to see what's in the box. There is money there and I think it better if he doesn't know about it.'

The manager still smiling, was now nodding sympathetically.

Jane hurried on. 'So, I would like you to stop him coming with me to the safe deposit room, keep him up here. Tell him only key holders are allowed down – something like that.'

She'd spoken throughout very slowly and clearly. Now she gave him an interrogative glance to see his response.

'Okay, I understand.' He replied in almost faultless English. 'You want that I should keep him up here while you go down with the key to look again in the box?'

Jane nodded and paused for a second. Then more briskly, she went on. 'I also want to hire another safety deposit box. About the same size as the box we have now. Do you have one available today?' She finished on a positive note.

The manager tilted his head back as if racking his brains. Then with his smile becoming even wider, he replied enthusiastically. 'We do. You come now for it?'

Jane nodded and they got up to tread the familiar path to the basement. A few minutes later they emerged and back at his desk, he filled out a form identical to the one she had found in her sister's baggage, down to the name and address of the hotel.

Jane left the bank thinking, 'That was easy!' There was now nothing left to do with the day but get through it painlessly. She thought about visiting Clarence, but decided she was not at that moment up for the emotionally exhausting, detailed discussions that would be unavoidable with the middle-aged dog lover, the lady of the kennels.

CHAPTER SEVENTEEN

Felix was also spending a lot of time in his hotel room, mostly reclining on his bed. It was that sort of hotel and that sort of room and it was hot outside. He'd spoken to Jane early in the afternoon of the previous day, after finding her mobile phone had been unavailable – maybe out of range for most of the morning. They were meeting in half an hour and Felix was nicely relaxed. He was always relaxed before any complicated piece of business because, as he would say, he'd done his home work.

They met in a café across from the bank. He was just finishing his coffee when Jane arrived, all flustered and attractive, exclaiming about a hair dryer that had refused to function properly.

'Maybe, it needs some kindness!', he said, demonstrating an irritating habit of adding sudden twists to conversations in the form of near *non sequiturs*.

Jane stared at him for a second, before saying, 'It gets quite enough love for what it performs,' and sitting down opposite him ordered a coffee. Once it arrived and she'd taken a few sips, she looked at him, raising an eyebrow, saying, 'Okay, what now?'

'Here it is! We go into the bank and I give you the key and we go to wherever their deposit room is and we open the box and I look into it; see what's there. Okay?'

In answer, Jane simply held out her hand. Felix looked blank for a moment and then with a start, pulled out his wallet and extracted the key he had killed her sister for. He handed it over and Jane glanced at it, noting it had indeed the correct number, before stowing it away in her handbag and returning wordless to her coffee.

Inside the bank, they stood looking around for a moment, Jane allowing Felix to both orientate himself and lead the way, not wanting to give the idea she knew the place. Almost immediately he started edging towards the manager's open-plan office. Jane followed. The bank manager looked up, a non committal expression on his face until he saw Jane. Then he smiled, but no more than he might at any pretty young girl, Jane was relieved to note. Indicating empty chairs on the other side of the desk, they both sat down.

Jane leaned forward and with a demure little smile said: 'I have a safety deposit box here and we would like to look into it,' emphasising the 'we'.

For a second the manager's face was blank and then he smiled broadly and said. 'You are the key holder? Then follow me!' He got up and came round his desk, heading for the door at the back of the office.

They both followed him, Felix first. Jane's heart sank and she started to panic until the manager turned and, still smiling broadly, put his hand onto Felix's chest to stop him.

'Only the key holder, I am sorry!' and he waved Jane past. Before Felix could gather what was going on, they'd both gone through the door to the basement steps. It clicked firmly shut in Felix's face.

Down in the basement the manager went to the little desk at the far end of the room. Jane followed him and duly proffered the key with the receipt. Still smiling broadly he picked up a ledger and made an entry while she stood patiently watching him. Then gesturing for her to go to the box, he turned his attention to firing up a computer.

Jane went over to her sister's box alone, pulled it open and lifting out the briefcase, which she put on the floor, stood silently for a moment surveying the cardboard boxes overflowing with hundred dollar bills.

She then delved into her handbag and took out the key for the box she'd rented the day before. As she opened it, she glanced back at the manager to see if he was watching her. He looked up from the computer, nodded encouragingly and returning to the ledger, made an entry recording that she'd opened a second container as well.

Jane realised they were quite systematic about their records in this bank. Where is the famed Spanish informality and carelessness when you need it? She thought.

Quickly she got down to transferring the cardboard boxes full of hundred dollar bills to the new one. Eventually, all that was left was the brief case. Removing her sister's papers from it, plus the passports, she returned it to the old empty deposit box.

Jane reflected that she was now in the same position as a sudden lottery winner. Although, of course, a lottery winner's position was several leagues safer.

Putting the new safety deposit key in a small compartment in her handbag so it would not be confused with the one Felix had given her, she strolled across to the desk as the bank manager rose to meet her. 'All finished, Senorita?' he said.

Jane nodded and they made their way back across the floor and up the stairs to the bank proper. Felix was hovering close to the door, an expression impossible to decipher darkening his face. Jane smiled at him brightly and saying goodbye to the manager over her shoulder, led Felix out of the bank and into the street.

Outside she shook her head dolefully, a long expression on her face.

'Well, that was a waste of time. We got down there and got to the box and then he asked for the receipt and when I hadn't got it, he wouldn't let me go any further. Why he couldn't have told us that in the bank and saved us all that palaver, I don't know. They have no respect for other people's time here in Spain.'

As she finished speaking, she looked fully and frankly into Felix's face.

'But you were a long time there. What were you doing? It was at least ten minutes!'

'Well, first he had to take my name and address and enter it in a register and then when I hadn't a receipt, he went into a long circular explanation about how I would have to go to a notary or someone like that and swear an oath that I was who I was and that I had lost his blasted piece of paper. Then, when I asked him if I could have a look anyway, he went into an equally long explanation of why I couldn't. I mean to say, talk about bureaucracy...' and Jane trailed off in apparent exasperation.'

There was a long silence as Felix digested what she had said.

'So, what do you want me to do now?' she asked, giving Felix an inquiring look.

'Well let me pay you first,' and he handed her several euro notes folded together. 'I think you'll find that correct. And for the moment I'll have to think about things – I'll let you know. Give me a couple of days and I'll call you. Okay? You'll still be here, won't you?'

In answer, Jane nodded and after a few more words, they parted, Felix to his hotel and Jane to a beach bar for a much needed drink.

CHAPTER EIGHTEEN

Both needed to think. Jane, on the face of it, had less of a conundrum to deal with. If broken down to its constituent parts, it came to simply leaving town with the money and the dog. And she was in two minds about the dog, now being tempted to give the kennels a big fat fee to find Clarence a 'good home'.

Felix on the other hand was coming as close as he ever had to thinking that maybe he could have handled things better. What particularly annoyed him was that his plan of action once they had arrived at the bank was, on examination, no plan at all. He'd stood there while this young and virtually unknown woman had left for the safe deposit room with the key to the box containing all his money. Money he'd already killed twice for and was now in the act of double crossing his only trusted, long-time associate. He faced the ruins of years of work at the very least, without considering what other retribution might await him.

He had the key back and now knew that the safe deposit receipt was also needed to confirm the original lease holder's identity, he supposed. It was plain that everything still focused on the bank and that was where his efforts must be directed. He now doubted if employing an Emma look-alike had been a good idea, although at the time it had seemed so perfectly apt, so perfectly planned!

It was, at the worst, beginning to look like some sort of poetic justice levelled at himself, while his recent efforts appeared to be completely beside the point. He should have rented a deposit box himself first and gone through the procedure to discover exactly what had to be done to recover the original box.

Now, Felix realised he must start over again with the bank, but this time with expert help. He would find an interpreter to come with him and reveal everything. That was it. Suddenly tired, although it was still only the middle of the afternoon, he drifted off into a short siesta.

Later that afternoon, he went down to the hotel foyer and asked the lady behind the desk if she knew of a Spanish/English interpreter. Without answering, she leant over to a shelf behind the counter and handed him a card covered in adverts for various tradesmen and services, all in English.

Glancing quickly down, he zeroed in on the only advert for translation work. It said: 'For all translation, legal and courier service, including visits to hospitals and municipal town halls, all dealings with local bureaucracy, call Tracy.'

Felix took out a leather bound Filofax and extracting a gold filigreed pen, made a note of the number. Looking round for a phone to use, he thought it was about time he got a local mobile phone. It was criminally expensive to use his British mobile for roaming calls and, more importantly, he needed a number that couldn't be traced back to him.

Back in his hotel room, Felix lay on the bed again thinking that if there was going to be a particular memory of this trip to Spain, it would be lying endlessly on a narrow hotel bed. After some difficulty getting an outside line, he dialled Tracy's number. Almost instantly a fluting North American accent answered.

Felix began, 'I have your advert here and it says you are an official translator?' It was a question and Felix paused for an answer.

'Yes, that's correct,' Tracy answered and immediately began listing an academic career that should have spanned several lifetimes. Amongst the recital was a claim to have been Professor of Russian literature at Columbia University, New York, New York, as she put it.

Felix abruptly interrupted, 'I only want to go to a bank. I don't want a translation of Ana Karenina!' Realising this was not a good start if they were going to work together, he quickly followed with a laugh saying, 'Only joking, maybe another day I'll need a quick PhD on *The Idiot*.'

If he was trying to send up Tracy, he was wasting his time, the word bank had pressed another button. She ran on, 'I had to go to a bank yesterday with a client. I do a lot of banks. I used to work for a bank, not actually behind the counter. I did security for a major Toronto bank.'

She paused long enough for Felix to interject. 'You were a security guard for a bank as well!' Disbelief informing his tone.

'No. Not a security guard. I was in charge of security. An administrator – had an office and staff. I was responsible for all security to an area manager.'

'This was before you became professor of Russian literature? I must say, it's quite a change of pace - going from stopping people stealing the bank's money to guiding post graduates students to the more esoteric realms of nineteenth century

Mother Russia. Tell me, which was the day job?' Felix was beginning to enjoy himself.

Finally, catching his risible undertone, Tracy abruptly stopped speaking.

Felix continued, 'So, can we make an appointment to go to a bank with me and translate. I have a bit of business to do. It's the Solamar Bank.'

'Certainly.' Tracy replied, now at her stiffest. 'When?'

'Oh, it's too late today. I think they close at two, don't they? What about tomorrow? We could say 10 o'clock tomorrow morning then?' He paused, waiting for a response.

'Let me consult my Filofax.' Still very stiff, very formal.

I'm not going to be forgiven that easily, Felix thought. The pause continued long enough for Tracy to discover a small window in presumably the most crowded of diary pages and then she was back.

'Yes! 10 o'clock is fine. Shall I meet you outside?'

'No, across the street in the café opposite. We can have a coffee and get to know each other better.' Felix wanted to see whom he was dealing with.

They rang off and he felt a little better. Maybe he could make some headway using a professional and if she had half the experience she claimed they might know her in the Solamar bank and so give him some leeway.

Next morning Felix turned up early at the café and sat with a black coffee. Being sluggish that morning, he asked for three sugars to wake himself up, get the adrenalin going. When Tracy walked in, he knew it had to be her. Tall and dark with a big head and a bigger bottom, giving out a silvery little, 'look at me' laugh every few paces. Felix waved her over to his table. She gave him a smile that would have made bees swarm and sat opposite him.

'Would you like something? A cup of coffee,' he asked, looking around ostentatiously for the waiter. Noticing one leaning elegantly, crossed legged against the till, Felix stuck up a hand and the man heaved himself off the counter and came slowly over.

'I'll have a café con leche and maybe a magdalena,' Tracy said, looking across at Felix. She was smiling less brightly now, lapsing into a more subdued role.

Felix waited until the waiter had gone.

'I need a translator to go with me to the bank. That's all. It'll take maybe half an hour. What would your charge be for that?' Felix liked to establish costs in advance.

'Oh, I only work in blocks of one hour, so I will have to charge you for a whole hour.' The dazzling, skin deep smile had returned. 'It'll be thirty euros.'

Tracy ended in an almost triumphant note, as if she'd just pulled off something quite difficult.

Felix nodded. 'It is not your normal inquiry,' he explained. 'I'm investigating something a little out of the ordinary. It's about a safe….'

'Deposit box!' Tracy finished for him. She was nodding wisely. Felix's head came up fast, looking across at her with renewed interest.

'How did you know what I was going to say?' he asked after a few seconds. 'How did you come up with a safe deposit box? Or are you just finishing my sentences for me already?' He sat back in his chair, smiling warmly, waiting.

'Oh, I know all about safe deposit boxes. I was in that very bank,' gesturing towards the Solamar bank, 'only a few days ago with a young lady. She wanted to look in a box she'd lost the key to, and let me tell you, it was some sight. I don't think I've seen so much money in my life - except of course, when I was Head of Security for the First National Bank of Canada in Toronto.' She added hastily.

Felix was now staring at her as if he's seen a ghost. 'What do you mean, she'd lost her key? If she'd lost her key, they wouldn't let her look. I was only missing the receipt for the key. I had the key and they….'

Felix trailed off as the full, awful truth dawned on him. He'd only gone and given the key to a safe deposit box full of their money to the sister of the woman who'd stolen it in the first place, the sister of the woman he'd killed to get it back. That's who Jane must be, so of course, she'd already have the receipt for it. And he'd allowed her to go down into the bank vault alone! Ashen is the only word that now described Felix's face – ashen with a tinge of green.

Holding up his hand to stop the flow of reminiscence about banks and banking that was now washing across the table, he looked around for inspiration. He needed time to think. The situation was suddenly much worse and much more layered. The first thing to do, he realised, was to get this Tracy woman on his side. He had to understand the situation quickly, to get a handle on it. At the moment the goal posts were not so much moving, as dancing. He looked up, forcing a smile.

'I think I need your help on a slightly more permanent basis. Are you very busy now?'

Tracy was already shaking her head as he finished speaking.

'No, I have some things on at the moment, but nothing to stop me doing extra work for you!' Her enthusiasm was palpable.

Felix nodded automatically, still preoccupied, then looking back across at her, he asked: 'This other woman you took into the bank. Her name wouldn't happen to be Jane, would it?' He waited for an answer. The atmosphere was suddenly electric. Tracy was staring back at Felix and he could see from her tight expression that her brain was also revving up.

She nodded. 'Yes, her name was Jane. That's how she was introducing herself anyway...' and she trailed off.

Despite this potentially disastrous news, Felix found himself noting her curious syntax. Was this a glimpse into Tracy's own consciousness? Did she use other aliases? It was more likely that Tracy enjoyed several personalities under the umbrella of a single name. Several aliases would not work in such a small town, although multiple personalities seemed quite the norm, but never-the-less, he might need Tracy, someone obviously flexible, not too attached to silly old reality.

Felix needed time to think. He asked her precisely when they'd gone to the bank and it didn't take him long to realise that Jane's visit had happened between their first meeting and them going to the bank together a couple of days later. Now, maybe for the first time for Felix, other more sinister shadows than his own were shifting behind the arras. Totally distracted, he got up to leave, arranging to meet Tracy again in a couple of hours.

He was at a loss about what to do next. It looked as if Jane was indeed Emma's sister and she must have had the necessary paperwork to access the box with the key he'd obligingly supplied. She had obviously also arranged for his exclusion from the vault. The manager had disappeared down the steps with her, but there was nothing to say she had not been alone in the vault itself. And what about Roy, was he in on this, maybe working with Jane? It now seemed an appalling mistake to have let Roy escape in the first place.

Maybe he should go down to the Winking Frog right now – maybe Jane would be there, she'd already vacated her hotel (he'd checked that morning). Getting into a taxi, he directed it to take him along the beach road passed the bar. The driver set off so fast that Felix, with hand gestures, asked him to slow down. He didn't and seconds later, contrived to side swipe a fruit stall.

A furious row then erupted between the driver and several stall holders and Felix, in a mood that could have triggered a thunder storm, threw himself out of the taxi and pushing a few euros into the driver's distracted hand, left him arguing heatedly with the stall owners, now gathered in the middle of a growing and attentive crowd.

Passing the Winking Frog, he saw nothing of interest – the place appeared abandoned, sunk in gloom. He found another taxi and returned to his hotel, still no clearer on what he should do.

CHAPTER NINETEEN

Fifteen minutes later Roy arrived back at the Winking Frog so obviously preoccupied that Rita broke their protracted silence to ask what was the matter. Roy merely ignored her and passing through, went to sit at the bar where he lit a cigarette.

Rita joined him a few seconds later, lighting up herself, and they sat in silence until Roy said: 'You'll never guess who I just saw outside – well, a few streets away, anyway?'

Rita looked at him, but didn't answer; they had been married long enough to know the routine.

'Felix, the asshole in the Lake District.' Roy went on. 'The one I told you about who locked me in that cellar. Just saw him. He was in a taxi that hit a stall holder. There was a big row between the driver and the stall holders and he got out and walked away.'

Rita looked across at him in surprise. 'What's he doing here? Maybe you should turn him in?'

Roy's head shot up and, looking at his wife, began shaking his head. 'Oh Yea, and what was I doing in the Lake District in the first place?'

'Yes, what were you doing in the Lake District anyway?' she retorted. 'You were fucking both these fancy tarts and then when that Emma offered you all that money, you dived in headfirst, no questions asked about where it came from or anything!'

'It could have been legit...' Roy broke in.

But Rita cut in. 'Money of that amount can only be drugs - or drug related. Nothing else. You know that and I know that and the postman knows that. It always is! If he's here, then he's here and there's nothing we can do about it.' She paused.

'Anyway, I thought you were going to get the CCTV cameras working again? That's more to the point he's now in the vicinity. You keep on about crates of beer going missing all the time, so why don't you get onto it. You installed it, after all. It'll be the movement activated bit that's gone again and getting it going will be far more useful than going on about all the *might have beens*!'

And there the conversation ended and Roy, more to get away from his wife, picked up a tool kit and left to fix the TV spy camera system. He'd installed it himself, mainly to cover the bottle storage area outside, behind the building.

Twenty minutes later Roy was back to announce, 'I've fixed it – and it's not only working, but the camera's actually following you about again. Let's see what's been going on while we were away,' and he switched on the TV.

Being movement activated, the camera only came on when something changed within camera shot, so for a good twenty minutes Roy stood winding forwards past static scene after static scene. Just as he was about to give up and turn it off to format the hard drive and wipe the past out, real movement suddenly appeared.

Not much to begin with. On screen it was still the same bare and stationary back lot, but now a panel of light was defining the brick floor. They watched but it remained frozen and static until Roy was again about to switch off, when slowly into the shot, a ghostly grey figure of a man emerged.

A shadowy figure was moving slowly, bent over and dragging an inert figure by the legs. Plainly a woman and plainly dead. It was either Emma or someone who was wearing one of her favourite skirts, which had now wrapped itself back up nearly to her neck. Then just as they were about to disappear out of shot, the man suddenly stopped and straightened up, looking directly at the camera.

It was Felix. The definition was good enough for that. Roy leaned across and froze the film, then edged it back until Felix came back into full shot again. Simultaneously, a date and time appeared across the top right of the screen. Roy looked at his wife, almost beseechingly.

'That was a few hours after I left for England,' he said.

Rita studied it for a few seconds, then without speaking, gestured at the phone.

Roy, picking it up, dialled a number. Then in dog eared Spanish, asked to be put through to the Spanish police – the Civil Guard.

CHAPTER TWENTY

Jane settled back into her seat and stretched out her long, elegant legs. She looked round at the other people, finally allowing herself the luxury of relaxing after the last heart stopping days.

On the seat next to her was a local paper, the headline dominating the front page was about the arrest of a suspect after the body of a young woman was discovered in a local expatriate bar. She'd been identified as Emma Mallory, an English tourist, who'd worked there occasionally.

Fighting back the tears, Jane thought how she'd at least managed to get some revenge on her sister's killers – and hopefully, any attempt to wrest back the money would become a secondary issue to them as they fought off long prison sentences. They'd also be unlikely to own up to involvement with millions of dollars of drug money – for that was what it plainly was. This would give her a breathing space, a chance to disappear and make a new life for herself now that her sister, her only relative, was dead.

A polite voice asking what she'd like to drink, brought her abruptly back to her surroundings.

'Champagne. I'd like a glass of champagne,' she said, defiantly controlling her feelings. 'Champagne to celebrate.'

'Is this your first visit to Rio?' asked the air stewardess as she handed Jane an elegantly printed drinks menu.

'Yes.' She smiled, glancing through the list of fine, vintage champagnes. 'Yes, it is – for both of us.'

The stewardess looked puzzled for a moment as she glanced at the empty first-class seat next to Jane.

'Me and my dog Clarence,' Jane explained.

'He's in the hold!'

They both laughed.

The End...

Comments and reviews welcome
at: Costabooks.com